PR

THE INTREPID THREE

Winner: 2023 Speak Up Talk Radio Firebird Book Awards
in the Fantasy Category

"*The Intrepid Three* by Brianna and Matthew Penfold is a captivating science fiction adventure with profound themes woven into its intricate plot. The story's pacing is perfectly executed, with three narratives unfolding simultaneously as the tale progresses. Each protagonist—streetwise Dez, steadfast Walter, and innocent Arabella—is distinct and well developed, possessing unique abilities. The meticulously crafted setting is so immersive that it feels as though the reader has spent years in the three realms rather than the single day the story takes to unfold. With elements of faith and mythology seamlessly integrated into a fantastical universe, anticipation for the continuation of this saga will undoubtedly build as book one concludes. . . . Readers will find themselves wholly engrossed in the distant worlds of these three teenagers.

"Filled with surprises and thought-provoking content, *The Intrepid Three* will delight teen and young adult readers who enjoy exploring far-off realities. With its exceptional storytelling, perfect pacing, and richly developed setting, this first installment offers a tantalizing glimpse into a wondrous world that is sure to captivate readers."

—Literary Titan

"*The Intrepid Three: Animus Revealed* is a captivating fantasy adventure from husband-and-wife duo and debut authors Brianna and Matthew Penfold. This is a fast-paced, action-packed novel for young adult readers, set within three unique and different dystopian worlds. Each world is fascinating, and the book explores some of the key threats to our own humanity: the influence of big technological corporations, and the exploitation of human labour; the pervasive and invasive power of social media; and the growing wealth inequality which threatens our democracy. The characters are interesting, each from a different background with different life experiences. I look forward to reading how the characters develop and how their powers grow in the next book. The book will appeal to young adult readers who enjoy adventure, fantasy fiction, and dystopian novels.

"As the first in a planned series, this book introduces the reader to the three worlds, the three main characters, and the backstory of Pax. The book ends on a gripping cliff hanger, and I look forward to reading the next installment."

—5-Star Readers' Choice Review

"*The Intrepid Three* by Brianna and Matthew Penfold is a highly imaginative story that . . . brings a whole new meaning to our world. I love how the relatable characters, who all come from different walks of life, work together to drive the story through the chaotic battle between Author and Author's adversaries. This interesting cast reveals that embracing differences in others can create the most remarkable friendships. . . .

"[This is] a wild showdown between good and evil that keeps you wondering what will happen next and who will be the victor. I highly recommend it to any young adult or adult who loves a fantasy story that can't be put down."

—Amy Raines, 5-Star Readers' Favorite

"*The Intrepid Three* is a compelling and thought-provoking novel that will leave readers reflecting on the consequences of unchecked corporate power and the importance of human connection in a dehumanizing world. The well-drawn characters, vivid settings, and engaging writing style make it a captivating read. Fans of dystopian fiction and social commentary will find this book a thought-provoking addition to the genre. Overall, *The Intrepid Three* is a gripping and powerful read that will stay with readers long after they turn the last page."

—Margie Przybylski, Pacific Book Review

"I must say, this is a compelling fantasy novel from husband and wife authors Brianna and Matthew Penfold. . . . I had a blast with this book. I loved the characters, particularly Walter, and I enjoyed the growing threat that's never far away from the storytelling. . . . The writing style of the authors is spot on for young adult readers; there's plenty . . . happening all of the time, and the plot is, well, clever, and very unpredictable—the way a YA fantasy should be.

"So, I'm very happy to recommend *The Intrepid Three* to readers . . . who enjoy skillfully plotted, gritty novels populated with distinct and very memorable characters."

— 5-Star A Wishing Shelf Book Review, www.thewsa.co.uk

"Brianna and Matthew Penfold have created a superbly engaging work of young adult adventure that ties both science fiction and fantasy attributes into a concise and enjoyable story. I found the introduction to the different worlds and technologies interesting, especially as it provides a fair bit of social commentary by holding up a mirror to our tech-obsessed planet. The way that each character is shaped by their experiences worked well to add different personalities and unique skills to the plot. I enjoyed Arabella's emotional journey the most, coming from a place of privilege and having to face a pretty tough reality check. Each of the characters offers something for readers to relate to. *The Intrepid Three* is a highly recommended read and a great addition to any young adult fan's shelf."

— K.C. Finn, 5-Star Readers' Favorite

"The battle of good versus evil, light versus dark, is as old as time. Brianna and Matthew Penfold seamlessly integrate the classic theme in this riveting tale about three young heroes finding themselves at the center of momentous events upon which the fate of humanity resides. *The Intrepid Three* is deliciously unpredictable, strikingly relevant, but above all, an absolute belter of a novel. E- Corp seemed like a nod to Sam Esmail's hit television show, *Mr. Robot*. I enjoyed the distinct backgrounds and personalities of the three heroes and their unique powers. The character of Author also brings a layer of mystery to the story that adds to its charm. Overall, a brilliant start to a new series."

—Pikasho Deka, 5-Star Readers' Favorite

The Intrepid Three:
Animus Revealed
by Brianna & Matthew Penfold

© Copyright 2023 Brianna & Matthew Penfold

ISBN 978-1-64663-979-3

Published by

◤ köehlerbooks™

3705 Shore Drive
Virginia Beach, VA 23455
800-435-4811
www.koehlerbooks.com

THE INTREPID THREE

animus revealed

BRIANNA & MATTHEW PENFOLD

VIRGINIA BEACH
CAPE CHARLES

To Oliver, our very own little lumen.

PROLOGUE

BEFORE TIME, EVERYTHING was pitch-black, except for a lone bright light in the expanse. Suddenly, the light flared. Then again. On the third flare, there was a great explosion. Elements fused into the cosmos—stars, planets, and galaxies. Life sprang in the wake of the emanating wave. Remaining at the center of it all was the original light.

The light named each celestial body. One star, Calamus, the most brilliant, was plucked from its arrangement in the universe. It was chosen for a special purpose—the instrument to write the future of all humanity. The star was effortlessly fashioned into a long sliver of light resembling a pen, and the all-powerful light wrote into the darkness. Showing careful attention, the light shone over a world called Pax. Calamus was used to create the most beautiful home imaginable for the Paxians. Life expanded as flora and fauna flourished. After a long passage of time, which was only a flash for the light, it wielded Calamus again, forming the most beloved cast—people.

The light's paramount act of love was to place a piece of Calamus in human hearts. While the light was the original creator, Calamus permitted humans to create by their will, for better or worse.

1

EUPORIA MONDAY 7:50 A.M.

THE WORLD WAS full of concrete, glass, and steel. In Euporia, the distant sun, a rare acquaintance, peeked only above the tips of the skyscrapers once a day. There was almost always a slight drizzle landing on the sea of bustling black umbrellas and the exhausted arms attached. The smog sat heavily on the horizon while pedestrians swarmed in and out of the skyscrapers and donned their white E-Corp uniform, black E-Corp umbrella, and black E-Corp satchel. None of the apparel was without each person's employee identification number prominently displayed. The masses did not lift their heads, seemingly oblivious to the flocks of helicopters dropping off Management on the rooftops of each steel giant.

"Hurry up and scan your badge. It's not like you have all day," an unempathetic guard, only known as EC0139259, shouted his familiar greeting at the fifteen-year-old Dez. The teenager's hazel eyes no longer held their youthful glow. Like most children in Euporia, Dez Gibbous was forced to grow up early and begin her monotonous career.

Her bland E-Corp uniform looked as though it could swallow up her skinny five-foot-eight frame, so she used an extra belt to force the unappealing garb around her slim waist. Makeup was expensive in Euporia, but even if Dez could buy some, she wouldn't have used it. It was too much work on top of an already suffocating schedule. Her short and stick-straight brown bob was just as low maintenance as her facial routine.

Dez often wondered if EC0139259 was able to say anything else. And just like every day, she didn't move any faster, knowing that her twelve-hour shift would be just as tedious as yesterday's. Moving through the scanner, the Loyalty Building opened to a large atrium filled with dozens of glass elevators. Dez shuffled over to wait in the queue for elevator C, with all the other hundreds of coders that worked on floors thirty through forty-nine.

Climbing aboard, Dez and twenty other coders waited for their daily motivational briefing. As the elevator started to ascend, a programmed holographic image of the brightly dressed CEO of E-Corp appeared on the panes of the elevator glass. The cheery voice boomed through the occupants' employee identification numbers and paused after each to comment on their productivity ratings.

"Good morning, EC3315763." Dez nervously listened as her statistics were read to the entire elevator, knowing she was dangerously close to being reprimanded. The voice didn't lose its upbeat cadence while reading Dez's dismal numbers. "You are currently performing at a 2.1, which is 0.3 down from last week. E-Corp looks forward to you improving your productivity. Remember, you are a valued member of the E-Corp team, but you are replaceable."

Most of the other occupants' numbers were above 3.5, a very safe tier to find oneself. The highest potential rating was a 7.0, but this was impossible to achieve. Management made sure of that with their rigged algorithm.

Productivity in the eyes of Management was the only thing that mattered. Above 2.0, managers left their employees alone, but below 2.0, managers began to take action at their own discretion. Discipline almost always meant firings, and firings almost always meant becoming a Forgotten.

The Forgotten had no place in the E-Corp world, and if a person had no place in the E-Corp world, they had no place at all. They resided stories deep below the bustling city where the only light was flickering flames. In Euporia, value was equivalent to the floor you lived on; the Forgotten lived and worked in negative numbers.

"Thirty-third floor," chimed the elevator as Dez's checks flushed red from embarrassment. She did not know why she felt humiliated in front of the other passengers; she didn't know them, nor did she care to. The reclusive girl's detachment from her peers was unspoken company policy. E-Corp frowned on friendships in the workplace, and even acquaintanceships were discouraged. Few addressed each other by name.

Nevertheless, Dez felt ashamed of her consistently low productivity ratings. She spent much of the day distracted by the deteriorating health of her parents, Ada and Leo Gibbous. Like many middle-aged Euporians, Dez's parents suffered from Euporian Exhaustion. This chronic disease came from working twelve-hour shifts, six days a week, fifty-two weeks a year for decades. The hallmark symptoms of the disease, profound fatigue and deep depression, robbed the afflicted of any quality of life. Her parents spent their days and nights shut-in their convalescent studio apartment.

Dez stepped out into a sea of cubicles. The scent of hopelessness filled the stuffy air. Her tiny workstation was crammed in the back corner, which would be tolerable but for the blacked-out windows. E-Corp deemed views of the outside world a distraction and waste of company time, thus decreasing productivity. Dez placed her fingers on the keyboard while a bright flash of light scanned her fingertips. The monitor opened automatically to the previous day's repetitive task.

"Ugh." She let out a stifled, exasperated sigh. Dez knew that she must code five superfluous new E-Corp products for the website before leaving for home. All of this work had the potential to increase her productivity to only a 2.5. If she wanted to get to a 3.0, Dez would have to code at least ten new products within the next twelve hours. Dez wondered if she was doomed from the beginning.

In Euporia, E-Corp determined everything, even a person's fate. All children were tested at the age of thirteen with the PLACE

(Personal Labor Aptitude Calculator Exam), to determine their station in the world. Each child was marched into one of the many E-Corp testing centers for a fifteen-minute imaging brain scan. During testing, one child after another was wheeled on a gurney into a narrow and dark imaging machine, converted from an MRI scanner. While in the claustrophobic tube, an E-Corp scientist read aloud a series of hypothetical scenarios involving management, technology, and ethics topics.

As each child answered the questions, various regions of the brain produced different colors for the E-Corp scientists to measure. Children testing primarily red were deemed to have leadership characteristics and were sourced into Management, while children testing primarily blue were deemed to have technological skills and were sourced into Technology. Five percent of the time, children tested primarily yellow, which indicated neither management nor technological aptitude. Being deemed useless to E-Corp, they were sent below the city to live as Forgotten. To maximize productivity, most other tasks in Euporia were performed by automated machines.

Dez grew cold and her heart raced as she thought back to her testing day. The last scenario she was presented still haunted the world-weary fifteen-year-old. *"If your mother was about to be sent underground to the Forgotten, would you (a) try to buy her position back, (b) hack her records to fabricate her productivity ratings, or (c) ask to take her place,"* read the cold scientist.

Dez answered, *"I would—"*

BEEEEEEEEEEEEEEEEP.

As with all the other questions, Dez was not able to finish her response before the machine recorded her answer. *"Thank you,"* interrupted the scientist donning a perfectly pressed white lab coat. *"Your answers were registered, and you will receive the results of your scan in forty-eight hours. You must report to your assignment within one day of receiving your results."*

In retrospect, Dez should have known her answers would

lead her to Technology. She was not callous enough to place in Management, and she imagined the brain scan revealed this truth. Dez also attributed her rejection of the harmful system designed by the monopoly to her parents. Unlike most adults, her parents lived open-eyed to the reality of E-Corp's oppression.

Many parents lived within the unchallenged, rigid rules of E-Corp and taught their children to follow suit. Apps controlled by the company were commonly used to arrange marriages. These apps were particularly popular because most people did not have time to date due to their grueling work shifts, and socializing at work was forbidden. The apps supposedly calculated the risk of a couple's offspring testing red, blue, or, God forbid, yellow. An individual uploaded the results of their childhood brain scan, and the app matched that user to another user with the highest likelihood of producing Management offspring.

Matched marriages were not the only way to source children into Management. Many guardians hired expensive E-Corp "placement coaches," sometimes spending a year's wages, to train their children into beating the impending brain scan. Dez's parents refused to buy into either of these carefully manufactured scams, apps or coaches, as they knew both measures were manipulated to create employees for their dominion. Even with this knowledge, Dez's family, like all Euporians, were still vulnerable to the dangers of the greedy behemoth.

E-Corp was formed nearly a century ago. Over that time, the giant perfected control and apathy. Through shady business dealings, financial ruses, and labor exploitations, E-Corp pushed out all other corporate competition. Everyone was now dependent on E-Corp as they were the main manufacturer, seller, and employer in Euporia. The small Euporian government did nothing to regulate the large enterprise. Management had infiltrated the administrations long ago.

Dez's computer screen flashed bright red; she had not pressed a key in five minutes. This was another one of the daily motivational reminders implemented at the workplace. Of course, there were no managers actually on the floor to motivate, but their presence was always felt. Rotating cameras lined the ceilings, and every computer's camera was permanently activated. Dez wondered if there was anywhere in the building safe from Management's eyes. Sometimes, she would make goofy faces in the bathroom mirror, hoping to remind the managers, and herself, that she was just a kid.

Her fingers hurriedly dashed across the keyboard as she began coding. Each techie was expected to enhance the E-Corp website product page with cheap, everyday items. The only competition for the massive conglomerate was the Forgotten-run black market. Rebellious citizens of Euporia would risk their lives and livelihoods to buy a wide range of higher quality products from the black-market vendors. Dez understood E-Corp's interest in productivity was really about controlling consumers and increasing profitability. Premature obsolescence was the name of the game for the massive company. The more often things broke, the more often they had to be replaced.

In the past, Dez coded mediocre E-Corp products from toilet paper to appliances. She was working on Vac-Trition meals, the most common and affordable vacuum sealed meals in Euporia. If there was ever a question of E-Corp's depravity, these meals were evidence. It was her impossible job to make these almost inedible brown, moist mounds seem appetizing. There were different flavors, but in reality, the meals all looked and tasted the same. The only reason people purchased Vac-Trition was because fresh food cost an exorbitant amount.

Suddenly, the blacked-out windows turned into a live video feed. In view was the floor manager, Ms. Mayflower. Her name was fitting since she always dressed in floral pantsuits. "Good day, darlings," rang out Ms. Mayflower. Her employees found this pet name to be more demeaning than endearing, especially since she almost never made an appearance on the floor. "Our esteemed CEO, Mr. Rothchild, has a special message for you today. But first, I would like to remind everyone that our productivity numbers are stagnant, and we must always strive to be better, better, better than before."

Ms. Mayflower abruptly disappeared and was replaced by a video feed of Mr. Rothchild in his extravagant office. White-haired and pale, Mr. Rothchild dressed in an expensive teal suit with an orange bowtie and pocket square, which, despite the brash color combination, was perfectly tailored. Mr. Rothchild's large stature and bright attire made for a blinding and frankly ridiculous sight. The employees on floor thirty-three paid special attention, as this was a rare instance to see the CEO on a live feed.

"At E-Corp, we take great pride in our image. Over the last month, our productivity levels have steadily declined, and it's not going unnoticed by anyone. I wouldn't be surprised if even the Forgotten have heard about it." Dez could hear whispers from the surrounding cubicles of her coworkers discussing their steady or increased productivity ratings. She knew that while her personal numbers had decreased in recent weeks, the company as a whole was outperforming last year's productivity average and was more profitable than ever.

The CEO continued, all the while with a fake smile. "Due to this slide in your standards, E-Corp is initiating a new and improved motivational campaign. As you all know, we previously corrected course when individual employee productivity ratings fell below 2.0. You'll be glad to hear that Management will now assist you if you fall below a 3.0."

Dez, along with the other employees, wondered how this system could be new or improved. As the helicopter warmed up on the landing pad outside of the twenty-foot-high wall of windows, Mr. Rothchild ended his message with, "I am a very busy man, so I'll leave you with this last thought. Another testing day is next week, and we will soon have new and eager employees on your floors. Remember, you are a valued member of the E-Corp team, but you are replaceable." The live feed faded out, the opaque windows returned, and all the computers on floor thirty-three flashed red.

Anticipation was almost palpable as the Murk looked on from Animus. The creatures knew that as the fear-driven evil actions of Euporians multiplied, so did the number of Murk. There were so many Murk amassed watching the scene unfold, they could not believe their presence wasn't felt by the citizens of Euporia.

2

AURELIA MONDAY 8:18 A.M.

THE WORLD WAS full of sunlight, green spaces, and mansions on every street. In Aurelia, with every increase in block number, the houses became impossibly grander. While there was an obvious distinction in wealth, the lowest Aurelian did not want for material possessions. On the meticulously curated sidewalks, people walked along with smiles on their faces, pet leashes in hand, and a friendly greeting for every passerby. The beautiful people proudly wore clothes embroidered with the Aurelian flag, an emblem of a bright-gold sun rising against a navy-blue sky. Every sight was picture-perfect.

At 1000 Golden Ray Avenue sat the largest home in Aurelia. A stone wall enclosed the vast estate. A black iron gate was the only point of entry to the gigantic stone manor. Luxury cars lined the semicircle driveway, and undoubtedly even more expensive cars filled the detached garages.

"Pull back on the reins, Arabella," reminded Mr. Penderbrook, her riding coach. In the early morning light, Arabella's golden-brown skin shimmered with sweat. Her black hair shone in the bright sun; the light revealed natural blond strands strewn throughout her black locks. She felt out of character in her riding attire, as she was far more comfortable in a monochromatic A-line dress.

Even though Arabella was naturally beautiful, she still awoke early every morning to follow the customs of Aurelia, a detailed face and hair regimen. Arabella wore a full face of makeup and a highly styled wavy updo. She was a typical Aurelian fourteen-year-old, struggling to focus on what she was doing at eight in the morning after spending far too much time on her morning ritual.

On Mondays, Wednesdays, and Fridays, Arabella was scheduled for mandatory riding lessons. The national pastime was caballian pageantry. These caballi were not your typical horses, though. Aurelian caballi, commonly known as Monarchs, spanned eight feet high, twelve feet long, and weighed about two thousand pounds. Mastering this sport was very difficult because of the temperamental nature of Monarchs. For most, it took years of dedicated training to grasp even the most rudimentary skills of mounting and trotting.

Arabella was introduced to caballian pageantry at the age of five. Onyx had been her personal Monarch for the last nine years. He was given to Arabella on her fifth birthday, before she could even reach the hanging reins. Onyx's coat shared the same black with blond highlights of Arabella's hair. The petite teenager did not care much for competition, but Onyx made the sport well worth it. The Juniors Championship was weeks away, and as a daughter of one of the heads of state, she was expected to place.

"Hey, look! It's Arabella Rey!" yelled a tourist riding atop a double-decker bus going by. The tired teen wasn't the only person up at this hour. As long as the sun was up, there was a constant flow of tour buses to sneak a peek at the family home or, even better, one of its residents. Wanting to avoid gawkers, Arabella set up for her last pass before breakfast.

The small teen gave a gentle tug on the ornately jeweled reins around Onyx. The caballus bowed its tremendous, adorned head to the ground, practicing its salute. With a firmer tug on the extravagant reins, Onyx sprung forward into a steadily quickening pace. The duo maneuvered effortlessly around tight turns, through suspended hoops, and over impossibly high apices.

After the pass, Arabella hopped off Onyx, and the beautiful beast bowed as if knowing the significance of the child's Aurelian heritage. The rider placed her slight hands on the mammoth caballus's ears, and rested her forehead on his. "It's time for breakfast. Yours is waiting for you too. I'll miss you, friend. Until Wednesday." They both closed their eyes, and Arabella took a deep breath before parting ways with her companion. The small teen looked over her shoulder and smiled at the massive animal that appeared built for something more than just prancing.

Arabella made her way inside and navigated the endless hallways to the dining room. On the table sat an array of breakfast platters. She wondered why so much food was made for her family every day when only three people actually dined in the house. In perfect posture at the head of the table sat her mother, Benjamina. The girl adored but feared her mother. That dichotomy had only grown since her father died unexpectedly four years earlier.

Sitting next to Benjamina was Arabella's twelve-year-old brother, Maximillian. Beside his chubby frame and combed-over hair, the brother was a spitting image of his sister. Despite their frequent attempts to annoy each other, the siblings were best friends.

"Good morning, Arabella. Come sit down next to me." Benjamina spoke hurriedly to her daughter.

"Good morning, Mother. Good morning, Maxi Poo." Arabella sarcastically whispered at her brother as she walked by him.

"You know I hate that name," he loudly retorted as he flicked a piece of syrupy cinna-stack her way. Arabella swatted the flying Aurelian breakfast bread onto the floor.

Benjamina glared at the children. "I won't have this disgraceful etiquette at my table. Apologize to each other. I have a very busy day ahead of me, and I don't want to hear any more fighting. You need to behave." Benjamina quickly got up from the table, having barely touched her breakfast.

As always, she wore a fitted navy dress with a large Aurelian flag stitched over her heart, her black hair slicked back in a bun, and her gold signet ring on her right ring finger. Benjamina's appearance rarely changed, but since her husband's death, streaks of gray hair had multiplied, and slight bags had developed under her eyes. Arabella watched as her mother left the room, and she wondered how someone so diminutive could be so commanding.

The door to the dining room was quickly shut by one of Benjamina's bodyguards. Even though Arabella could no longer see her mother, she knew the powerful woman was off to help lead the country as national financier. Her mother was one in a long line of family members to hold that position over the past fifty years.

Arabella did not know the origin of her family's power, but most people in Aurelia did. The true money and power of Aurelia was controlled by an elite group of families, including Arabella's. These oligarchs passed money from generation to generation, and with each passing generation, the wealth compounded, along with their power.

In Aurelia, elections were held every five years, but most candidates ran unopposed. The same surnames appeared on the ballots year after year because the cost to register as a candidate was exorbitant. Only the wealthiest families in Aurelia possessed enough money to run for office.

The citizens of Aurelia seemed content with this system, or at the very least accepted its inevitability. There was no reason to protest because the powerful seemed benevolent and frequently bestowed gifts on all Aurelians, perks such as vacations, furniture, and, if necessary, cars. As long as life remained easy and light, no one complained or challenged the status quo. Providing comforts eliminated the desire by common citizens to strive for better, discover more, or excel beyond average.

Maximillian and Arabella polished off their decadent breakfast and pushed in their chairs. The children left their dirty dishes behind, knowing the house staff would instantly be behind them to clear their mess.

"Did you get your homework done?" asked Arabella.

"You know I never do my homework. It's so boring. I'll do my homework when they let me get my hands dirty. I'm so tired of having to be a stiff," responded Maximillian.

The two siblings couldn't have been more different. Arabella always completed her assignments on time. She feared the retribution of their private teachers and the inevitable disappointment of their mother. Maximillian, on the other hand, seemed to care much less, or at all. Maybe it was because he was twelve, or maybe he was just more self-assured.

Maximillian walked obstinately slow while Arabella dragged him along to the north wing of the house for their daily lessons. Mr. Flores, a man of average build with a sharp tongue, was waiting impatiently outside the classroom. His brown eyes peered down his long nose and through his thick spectacles at the approaching pupils.

As he tapped his foot, Mr. Flores said, "Class should have started one minute ago. You know the rule, every minute late is an extra homework assignment." As Arabella cast her eyes down, Maximillian snickered, knowing there were no consequences for the pair.

Arabella hurried into the classroom and took her seat closest to the teacher's podium. Maximillian begrudgingly took his seat behind his sister. The big room was full of floor to ceiling bookcases stuffed with thousands of matching leather-bound titles. Behind Mr. Flores's podium stood a huge dry-erase board that still held some of yesterday's lesson on Aurelian Civics. Mr. Flores instructed the children to stand for the pledge. Arabella and Maximillian stood and turned their attention to the huge gold and navy-blue flag hanging from the rafters. In unison, they all recited, "Aurelia gold and free. There's nowhere we love as much as She. Fortune, abundance, and security. We pledge ourselves to thee."

Immediately after the pledge, Mr. Flores quickly erased the whiteboard and jumped into the morning lesson. Arabella barely had time to open her favorite notebook to begin taking tedious notes. Like most days, the lesson was slated for more Aurelian Civics, but today's specific focus was on the nation's finances. Arabella was excited for this topic; she hoped the lesson would give more insight into her mother's job.

Part way through the lesson, Arabella, the quintessential teacher's pet, raised her hand. "Mr. Flores, after everything that you've taught us, I think you would do a great job working for our mother's agency."

Mr. Flores quickly retorted, "Arabella, my family's ancestors do not appear on our nation's currency, nor do I have enough zeros in my bank account. Expertise only gets you so far in this country."

"What do you mean?" She was puzzled.

Mr. Flores quickly turned his back to his two students, but not before a look of frustration passed over his face, "That's a lesson for another day. Let's take a ten-minute break before we start our next section."

Arabella was back in her seat halfway through the break, while Maximillian plopped into his seat just seconds before the ten minutes were up. The morning lessons carried on until finally it was time for lunch. After eating a meal just as lavish as their breakfast, the siblings headed to the south wing for their music lessons.

Surprisingly, they arrived before their teacher, Ms. Bridgewater. The music room was filled with enough instruments to compose an orchestra, but Arabella took her seat at the black grand piano while Maximillian grabbed his drumsticks. The room was primarily made of glass, and the light bounced beautifully off the sheet music.

Arabella began to gently play her favorite melody, "A Daughter's Dance," a song her father taught her years ago. Every time she played this tune, Arabella recalled a different happy memory of her father, Caius. Today, she drifted into a recollection of the first time she performed a routine with Onyx. Her devoted father was there, as always, to watch and cheer her on. As soon as she finished, Caius jumped to his feet and yipped, *"That's my girl. I knew you could do it."*

Clicking shoes awoke Arabella from her memory. The daydreaming girl could hear Ms. Bridgewater approaching. She jumped to her feet with the sudden urge to be near her father again. The only way Arabella knew how to achieve this closeness was to sift through Caius's belongings that Benjamina moved into the basement shortly after his death. Uncharacteristically, Arabella slid out of the music room through the door closest to her while her music teacher entered through the door nearest her baffled brother.

The emotional child's feet carried her more quickly than she had ever moved before, as if something was pulling her to the basement. She ripped open the basement door and descended into the darkness.

The Lumen buzzed with excitement as Arabella reached the bottom step. Would she find what's hidden this time? There was a new and faint light in Animus that gave the bright beings hope. Almost impossibly, this fourteen-year-old girl reinvigorated the Lumen. They began to believe the spoiled and complacent Aurelians were not lost yet, and the Lumen might just have a fighting chance against the Murk. The guardians remained at their posts as they kept watch.

3

IMMERXIA MONDAY 8:31 A.M.

● ● ●

THE WORLD WAS full of cookie-cutter neighborhoods, telecommunication towers, and homes stuffed with a deluge of electronics. In Immerxia, life revolved around buying, posting, and sharing online. Every man, woman, and child had numerous ways to electronically connect with their fellow Immerxians. Automobiles, house appliances, clothes, and even toilets had internet links. All personal information was intentionally displayed for the world to see. If two people were outside at the same time, it's unlikely either of them would notice the other, as their eyes and thoughts were always focused on a virtual reality.

Walter Johnson, a seventeen-year-old, began to stir to a repetitive chorus of dings. His dark hands immediately grabbed and pulled his CommX8 off the nightstand. He quickly mashed the alarm's "I'm awake" pop-up icon on his latest communication device's touchscreen. This sent out an instantaneous notification to anyone that was paired to him online. As he rolled over in bed, his short, black, coarse hair barely stuck out from underneath the covers. He pulled off his blanket, lamented his average build, and wished his growth spurt had given him a couple of extra inches this past summer.

Before climbing out of bed, Walter mundanely scrolled through the exceptionally long list of morning posts shared by his e-quaintances until he reached his friends' favorite online personality,

@JerrickKnowsAll. Even though no one knew who was behind the persona, Jerrick's followers unwittingly adopted many of their beliefs based on @JerrickKnowsAll's flaunting representations. The social media mogul's page boasted tens of millions of followers, thousands of sponsors, and endless uninformed opinions.

> What's up, my Know It Alls?!
>
> Yours truly posted all last week about the planned statue of our terrible Mayor!
>
> What do you think about this monstrosity going up in downtown Immerxia?

Walter did not know much about local politics but knew everything about @JerrickKnowsAll's feelings on the topic. He tapped the comment box to see which of his friends had responded so far. Upon clicking, a five-question poll popped onto the boy's screen. Each question came with only two polarizing answer options. At the top of the poll was a bright-flashing button that said, *See what Yours Truly picked!* Walter mashed the option and read through all of @JerrickKnowsAll's choices. The teen decided to shelf the quiz, knowing he was still ignorant about the subject despite spending the last few minutes sifting through the useless content. He wondered if any of his hundreds of peers really knew enough on the topic to have an informed opinion. He doubted any of them clicked on the small, inconspicuous link that would take them to the "learn more" page about the monument.

Without wasting another moment, the groggy adolescent slid out of bed and walked to the bathroom to start his morning routine. As he entered the small space, his CommX8 display appeared on every window and mirror. The device tracked Walter's movements in the house and auto-populated updates for each awaiting task. He suddenly noticed the *I'm brushing my teeth* icon appear on every surface around him. Before sending out this update, he reflexively selected the type of toothbrush and toothpaste he was using. Walter knew if enough Immerxians saw, commented, or rated his VEX, a minute-by-minute update of daily life and thoughts, he could receive minimal, very minimal, compensation from the company he endorsed.

Compensation for VEXs, an Immerxian acronym for Virtual EXperience, was not common for Walter. In the past year, he received twenty cryptx, Immerxian cryptocurrency, into his bank account from various companies. Walter was not deterred by the minuscule amount, as this was the Immerxian's way of life. His loving parents, Wendy and Wayne, encouraged Walter and his three younger siblings, Wallie, Whitney, and Wade, to share their earnings to help offset the high cost of living in Immerxia.

Wayne and Wendy Johnson co-owned Vision Optix. Wayne was the practice's optometrist and Wendy worked as the optician. The business had a steady supply of patients due to Immerxians' twenty-four seven attention to screens, which created enormous eyestrain.

Despite the Johnson's success, the family still worked hard to keep each other comfortable in this expensive world. Every year, Walter's parents bought their three children the newest CommX devices. To make money, people needed to share, and share a lot. To maximize the capability to share, the latest technology was required. And technology was expensive. In Immerxia, people needed to spend money to make money.

Thirty-five VEXs later and no richer, Walter was ready for school. He quickly shared *Off to my first day of junior year* and selected his brand of backpack, hat, T-shirt, pants, and most importantly, shoes, in the dropdown menu. Walter didn't even bother to tell his parents that he was leaving, since he knew they would get his VEX before he even closed the door.

Once outside, each student that passed was a chorus of dings, bings, and rings as their clothes, school supplies, and CommX8s continuously alerted them of their peers' every movement. All around the children, there was a barrage of personal content displayed on every window in the neighborhood. Inhabitants freely shared their active screens, hoping to make extra cryptx from the passersby.

Walter suddenly saw that his shoes were glowing bright green. His sneakers were customized to light up when he received a geotag from one of his two best friends. The location of his friends scrolled around the outer sole of his shoe. Instead of walking to the bus, Walter darted ten houses down to Brian Watson's. In the driveway, Brian was leaning against a new blue car, an affordable Offbeat. He wore his shades down and showed a big grin. The car was no Xtender, the hottest car on the market, but it was the nicest ride any other junior in Immerxia owned.

Unlike Walter, Brian was a master at making cryptx off his VEXs. He had a knack for photography, original captions, and gaining access to top-of-the-line products, not to mention he was extremely popular.

"What took you so long to get here? I didn't want to VEX about my new car before you saw it. Now, I'm just waiting for Pete, and then I can share it with everyone."

"No way!" As if on cue, Pete Carrington, the remaining member of the trio, appeared around the corner. Brian and Pete were different in every aspect. Brian was muscular, athletic, and a straight-A student, while Pete was stout, a theatre kid uninterested in grades. While the two friends couldn't be more dissimilar, Walter had been best friends with both for ten years. He was the glue that kept the triad together, especially since Walter, the median of the three, could relate to both Brian and Pete.

"Alright, let's get on the road. I need to stop for a quick charge on the way to school. The car's battery came close to empty," Brian hurriedly stated. The boys quickly piled into the car. Walter graciously sat in the back and breathed in the new car smell. He was thankful to avoid the crowded school bus.

"Brian, don't you think we'll be late for first period math?" Walter asked over the wind of the open windows. "Nah, I can get us there on time," Brian responded as he pushed down the accelerator. "Do you think Mrs. Anderson would even notice if we came into class a few minutes late? She'll be glued to her CommX8 VEXing about the latest calculators and trying to make a few extra cryptx," Pete said with a snarky tone. All three boys laughed.

Many teachers, just as much as their students, spent most of the day on their electronic devices trying to make money from VEXs. Their classes were spent flippantly scrolling through lists of purchasable prerecorded lessons. Truthfully, educators in Immerxia didn't do much teaching. They were more like proctors. Once class started, a teacher's main role was to take attendance, press play to start the unoriginal lecture, and administer a few quizzes and tests each term. The hardest part of an educator's day was if a child interrupted the thoughtless routine with a question; they much preferred the students scroll silently on their electronic devices rather than speak up in the classroom.

As Brian pulled up to the charging center, Pete asked, "Did you guys hear the CommX9 is about to be released? I think it's really going to help boost my earnings. It's got ten cameras strategically placed to optimize VEX quality. Supposedly, one of the cameras can even produce 4-D images. It's like you're actually in the picture."

Brian retorted jokingly, "You're going to need the CommX20 to catch up with me." Brian jabbed Pete in the shoulder with his elbow after he unbuckled his seatbelt.

Before Pete could retaliate, Brian smoothly exited the car and started fiddling with the charging port. "Ah, man, this keypad is not working. Guess I'll pay inside with my CommX." Never missing an opportunity to grab a bite, Pete clumsily jumped out of the car and headed inside to grab some snacks.

Walter looked up from his device and realized he was alone. He was about to continue his unproductive scrolling when he saw something shoot past the windshield. Walter saw a spectral figure streak into the trees behind the charging center.

Walter had the bright idea to try to capture some images of the unique creature. While the phantom resembled a human, it was transparent, white, and its image flickered in and out of focus. Walter blinked hard twice, checking his vision. *Wait 'til people see this. I might actually be able to bring in some cryptx today,* Walter thought as he stepped out of the car with his device at the ready.

Walter slowly walked into the woods, in hopes of not spooking his prize, as the form flitted through the trees. Just as he was about to snap a picture, Walter's implausible subject disappeared toward downtown Immerxia. With Pete and Brian nowhere in sight, Walter decided there was enough time to chase this once-in-a-lifetime VEX. The form darted behind buildings down Main Street, always a block ahead of Walter. This sequence continued for seven blocks to the local library.

The Xitus Library was an old brick building that rarely welcomed visitors. Books were a relic in this world filled with technology. The last time Walter set foot in the library was his kindergarten field trip to see a book in real life. Now, the only people to set foot in the library were antique collectors—and apparently ghosts.

As Walter approached the seemingly deserted building, the phantom passed through the revolving library door, which did not even move an inch. Walter ran up the steps and burst into the building, instantly recognizing that the indoor setting was even better for his epic picture.

The teen carefully scanned for the VEX of the century as his eyes adjusted to the dim light. His vision focused with the help of the streams of light that snuck through the old two-story stained glass windows lining the entire perimeter of the Xitus Library. At least thirty twenty-foot glass masterpieces were in sight from the entryway. They spanned from the worn floor beams to the lofted ceiling trusses. Dust floated and swirled in the pale light, giving the dingy building an enchanted quality. The charmed atmosphere was mesmerizing.

Walter started to discern the vast open area full of archived books and antiquated desks but not a single electronic screen. He wasn't even sure if the building was equipped with basic electricity. Suddenly, Walter saw a burst of light to the right, and he jerked his head in that direction. The figure he followed to the end of town vanished behind the circulation desk.

Squinting his eyes, Walter noticed someone behind the desk. "What in the world was that?" Walter blurted. The presence leaned forward on the desk as if to get a better look at the boy. Walter peered back at the most interesting and indescribable being he had ever seen. Unlike most people, the figure possessed no distinguishing characteristics—no overt indication of gender, race, or nationality. All qualities seemed to be ambiguous to Walter. The boy was staring at what seemed like an optical illusion. In a moment, the librarian resembled any person; in another, no one at all.

"Hello, Walter. Sorry to ruin your VEX."

As Immerxians grew further distracted from truth, the unending battle continued between the Murk and the Lumen in Animus. The Murks' numbers were undeniably larger than the Lumens', and Animus had never seemed darker. The sheer numbers and darkness placed the Murk at an obvious advantage. The Lumen deployed to fight banded together to create pockets of bright resistance. The waves of darkness from the Murk crashed into the weakening Lumen. Unexpectedly, the Murk halted their assault. A bright light in the distance captured all the creature's attention. There could only be one explanation: something was being added to the story.

4

IMMERXIA MONDAY 8:49 A.M.

● ● ●

CONFUSED, WALTER ASKED, "How do you know my name? I've never met you before."

Chuckling, the figure responded, "I know much more than your name. I know that your favorite food is a pokit, but you only like them savory. I know your little brother Wade is your favorite sibling. I know Brian and Pete are wondering where you disappeared to this morning. But most importantly, I know this conversation will push you to question the vain lifestyle of Immerxians."

Walter froze, not comprehending how a stranger could know such intimate details about him. Sure, anyone could have guessed his favorite food was a pokit, the most VEX'd about Immerxian specialty entrée, but not even the CommX algorithm could have discerned the other details.

The larger-than-life personality continued speaking while exiting the circulation desk toward the boy. Trying to glean more information about the perplexing librarian, Walter scanned the being's attire. The outfit consisted of plain white sneakers, blue jeans, and a button-down shirt embroidered with a pattern of tiny *Xitus Library* logos. Fittingly, the emblems closely resembled the numerous stained glass windows adorning the walls. Unconcerned with the boy's growing wariness, the librarian stated, "Walter, you are set apart from your classmates. You are the best of them. I should know."

"Who are you? Do you track my VEXs or something?" Walter said, sounding increasingly nervous. A long silence ensued as they stared at each other. "Fine, at least tell me your name," Walter relented to break the quiet.

"Over time, I've been called many things, but my description has stayed the same. I find it is best to describe myself when someone meets me in person for the first time. I am the first light. Being the preeminent light, I am the author of all good things. Really, I am the most important author of all time. I create, continue, and complete the good text."

"Really? What text?" The boy was beginning to wonder about the speaker's sanity.

"I'm sure you've experienced my work. I authored everything from science and math to art and music. There's not a person in any world that has not lived my stories. My collection is really quite beautiful, if I do say so myself. Most people find my writing profound, except for those who choose to dismiss me as the author. Over the years, some of these people have tried to hijack or mar what I have written, but my voice endures," the author stated confidently.

"What's the title of one of your books?" Walter asked skeptically. This conversation was turning from weird to bizarre. He shifted his feet uncomfortably.

Needless to say, the foreign apparition was no longer at the forefront of his mind, and neither were the electronics that kept him tethered to Immerxian reality. Unbeknownst to him, Walter's shoes were repeatedly flashing green from the geotags sent by his friends trying to locate him.

"I wrote *Goodness*," the writer insisted.

Walter instinctively followed the being to a large wooden table with stacks of leather-bound books. "Okay. Well, what do I call you then?" the curious teen reasonably asked, feeling like his questions were leading nowhere.

"What would you like to call me?" the host replied.

"What have other people called you?" Walter asked, wanting a direct answer.

"That's unimportant. It matters what you want to call me," the odd librarian stated.

"I guess . . . I will call you Author, since you say you've written so much," Walter hesitantly said.

Laughing with enthusiasm, Author responded, "Good choice! I like it! Now, if you'll have a seat, I can tell you why you're here."

Walter gingerly slid into the seat across from Author and questioned, "Why I'm here? What do you mean?"

"You may not realize it, but the necessity for our meeting originated long ago. We all have choices, Walter. Even though I planned for your arrival, you've chosen to stay." Walter's face grew more confused with every passing word.

Walter scratched his head and stated, "The more you talk, the more questions I have."

As Walter squirmed in his chair, Author said, "Walter, you are one of my chosen."

Secretly searching for the nearest exit, Walter inquired, "Chosen for what?" The teenager had never seen himself as a leader or exceptional at anything.

Author gave him a benevolent smile. "You were chosen because of your ability. The ability to change everything."

"What special ability do I have? To change what? Everything? If you really knew me, you'd know I was average, and there is nothing unique about me. Brian's who you want. He's the smartest guy I know. Or, what about Pete? He can play any role you want," Walter suggested while he finalized his plan to escape from the incomprehensible situation.

"I hope Brian and Pete will play a part in all this too, but here is where you shine beyond your friends. I know you feel average most of the time, but you're far from that. You are designed to coauthor unbelievable wonders." Walter was suddenly distracted by an exquisite pen that appeared in the speaker's now outstretched hand.

Author continued undeterred by the mysterious materialization. "This world, and the others, need you. Immerxia is full of confusion because of the excess of information and inability to discern the truth. To most people, truth is now irrelevant. Veracity no longer is determined by fact but rather the whims of the loud and outrageous. You know this to be true because you have the capacity to see through all the commotion and chaos. This gift grants you the ability to materialize change for those that are still lost in the deception."

Walter abruptly rose from his chair, which toppled backward. "I don't know about all of this. I'm sure we have our problems here, but I don't think I'm the one to save us. Maybe run this by the next person who walks in here. I think it was a mistake for me to come in here today."

"No, my boy. There are no mistakes in my writing. No edits are necessary," Author proudly spoke.

At that very moment, Walter's CommX8 buzzed and caused him to jump, as if it was a planned disruption. Author, on the other hand, didn't budge or bat an eye. Nothing seemed to phase Author. The presence slowly rose from the chair and paused for the persistent buzzing of Walter's CommX8 to end before speaking again.

Once the racket stopped, Author continued, "I know this short chapter is ending, but I look forward to the next time we meet. You will discover that there is much more to you and this story than you could ever imagine. Much will happen before we meet again, and I'll be here to answer your questions."

Without another word, Walter turned and briskly walked out of the library, leaving Author standing alone at the table. Running down the stairs, Walter nearly face-planted while digging his CommX8 out of his pocket. There were ten missed messages.

Just as much as Walter had been bewildered, he was now elated to see not only had his best friends been searching for him, but so had Stacey, his unreciprocated childhood crush. Walter hoped this year would be the year that Stacey caught similar feelings for him.

His heart skipped a beat as he read Stacey's message. *Hey! Where are you? I got here early to save you a seat next to me in first period.*

On my way. Save my seat, Walter clumsily responded as he sprinted back toward the charging station, knowing his friends were still waiting for him.

Stepping from Immerxia into Animus, the Switcher's façade dissipated, leaving only an evil essence. While walking behind the ranks of the Murk, it was unaffected by the ongoing battle in Animus. Reaching a locus to Euporia, the Switcher parted the thin atmosphere. A large hand, gold watch, and French-cuffed wrist began to appear in Euporia as the Switcher emerged.

5

EUPORIA MONDAY 11:13 A.M.

THE MORNING'S EVENTS had weighed heavily on the frantic E-Corp workers of floor thirty-three. All that was heard across the workspace were frenzied fingers tapping across computer keys. Dez's fingers outpaced all the occupants of the surrounding cubicles.

Suddenly, her keyboard froze, and a pop-up appeared in the center of the already exhausted girl's screen.

OPTIONAL BATHROOM BREAK FOR EC3315763

11:14 A.M.

YOU HAVE ONE MINUTE.

Dez was thankful for the scheduled break. Every joint in her hands was aching from the barrage of typing. Dez linked her stiff hands in front of her and reached out. Each of her knuckles gave a loud synchronized pop. Ordinarily, the intrusive noise would garner a mean glare, but today, not even an air horn would distract the frightened employees.

Dez dragged past hordes of cubicles to get to the bathroom. She knew the one-minute time limit was the rule, and everyone obeyed, even though no Management was on the floor to enforce this allowance. Without regard to privacy, E-Corp located one restroom in the center of the floor, equidistant from every desk. Only one toilet was necessary on thirty-three as each employee was designated a minute every four hours.

Reaching the tiny and basic water closet, Dez swung open the lightweight door. She did not expect the sight before her. Seated on the tile floor was a thirteen-year-old girl. The child sat curled in an impossibly compact ball with her knees pulled to her chest. Tears streamed down her face onto her crisp white E-Corp uniform, the smallest uniform Dez had ever seen.

Even though all the occupants of the floor were absorbed with work, Dez chose to not react audibly. She did not want to draw any attention to the out-of-place child for fear of punishment for either of the girls. Dez was feeling shocked and annoyed that someone else was using her limited bathroom minute.

Dez quickly slid into the small room and closed the door tight behind her. "Umm, I think this is *my* minute."

The girl, with identification number EC3313554, did not respond and continued to cry into her chest. Her brown eyes welled and poured tears down her olive cheeks. Her long black hair fell in front of her bowed head like a curtain. The small girl's shoulders bounced up and down with each sob.

Understanding her moment of relief would not occur, Dez knelt and said, "Is this your first week? I know it can be overwhelming."

EC3313554 lifted her head and weakly nodded in affirmation.

Remembering the terror of her first week, Dez empathetically stated, "Fraternizing is against company policy, but despite E-Corp's attempts to micromanage us, we're still human. I'm Dez. What's your name?"

"I . . . I'm . . . Val. I'm . . . not sure if I . . . I can do this. My uncle already lives . . . underground. I . . . I should just go live with him," the desperate girl sputtered through her tears.

No one attempted to help the terrified Dez on her first days on floor thirty-three at E-Corp, so she contemplated leaving the pitiful

Val to cry alone on the slick gray floor. However, before Dez could further contemplate abandoning the other girl, Val proceeded with her plight. "I'm not even supposed to be here. My parents hired the best testing specialist in Euporia. I studied for months to beat the PLACE," Val spoke with a surprising amount of anger.

"Well, you are here now. There's nothing you can do about it. Take it from me, the best thing you can do is keep your head down. You start with a productivity rating of 5.0, so Management won't bother you anytime soon," Dez said, thinking her pragmatism would provide comfort.

Val's cries exploded into deeper sobs. Fearing attention from any nearby coworkers, which could attract attention from Management, Dez knelt on both knees and placed a hand on Val's shoulder to quiet her. "Sorry. I'm not very good at this. I don't interact with many people. Honestly, it does suck here, but I can tell you can do this job. If I can do it, so can you," Dez reassured, even though she was unconvinced herself.

The young girl's sobs turned to sniffles as her tears began to quell. With Dez's hand still on her shoulder, Val's posture relaxed. The thirteen-year-old's shoulders were still weakly slumped forward, but she pushed her legs straight out in hopes they would regain enough strength to carry her back to her cubicle soon.

Seeing Val's demeanor change, Dez further consoled with words a wise friend once told her. "This job does not define you, even though that's what E-Corp wants us to believe. We are more than a productivity rating, and we are more than our technology placement."

Dez lowered her voice, still unsure if their bathroom breaks were surveilled, and repeated an affirmation her parents had said to her every day on her way out the door. "Your value is deep. Your worth is immense." The teen felt a foreign smile form as she continued, "If you ever feel like this again, just know I'm in cubicle 763."

Continuing to test new phrases for the first time, Dez timorously stated, "You'll be my first work friend. It's time I start living outside of

E-Corp's boundaries, at least a little bit." During the silent moments that ensued, Dez was surprised how much she began to believe her own words. She was even more surprised that Val appeared to believe her monologue.

With confidence, Val stood. Dez's hand dropped from the rising girl's shoulder, and she stood facing her confidante. Both girls took a deep breath and steadied themselves for the coming hours.

"I don't know how, but I'm feeling somewhat better. You've helped me to be a little happy for the first time since my PLACE results. Maybe I *can* do this. I'm glad I have a friend here, especially you," Val stated, visibly changed.

Before opening the door to reenter the bleak E-Corp world, Val raised to her tippy toes, reached her small arms around, and embraced Dez. While squeezing the older girl, Val pronounced, "Friends."

Caught off guard by the show of affection, Dez froze with her arms outstretched. Relenting to the girl's hug, Dez spoke in a hushed tone, "And, allies."

Val gave a wave and exited the bathroom first. She quickly disappeared into the maze of cubicles toward seat 554. Never really needing to use the bathroom, only wanting a moment away from the clacking of keys, Dez opened the door a few seconds after Val and walked away from her only break of the morning. Thankfully, no one was impatiently waiting outside of the bathroom. The employees with the next bathroom breaks must have been so obsessed with their projects they decided to skip the time away from their desks.

After a few steps from the bathroom threshold, Dez saw Ms. Mayflower approaching from around a nearby workstation. The sight of the always absent manager stopped Dez in her tracks. Ms. Mayflower walked directly to the stunned teen and halted inches in front of her. The two were so close, Dez perceived the smallest, repetitive twitch of her boss's button nose. This involuntary flutter was imperceptible over the video messages.

The twenty-year-old Ms. Mayflower's lips were moving, but her words were nearly drowned out by the loudness of her appearance. She wore a floral hot-pink and highlighter-yellow pantsuit, which did not compliment her dyed bright-orange hair and bright-blue colored contacts. The manager and employee stood eye to eye at the same height. Along with their attire, the two differed in physique; Ms. Mayflower did not want for food like Dez.

"Darling? Darling! Did you hear me? Why aren't you at your desk? I believe your bathroom minute is well over," Ms. Mayflower interrogated.

Dez finally focused on the words of her boss and replied, "Uh, yes, ma'am. I'm heading there now."

The panicked adolescent made a beeline for her cubicle, but not before hearing Ms. Mayflower call out, "Oh, Darling. Remember, you are a valued member of the E-Corp team, but you are replaceable."

On the short trip back to her coop, Dez anxiously pondered, *Why is Ms. Mayflower on the floor? She's never on the floor. Is she here just for me? There's no way she's here just for me. How did she get here so fast? I thought her office was floors away. Am I going to be punished for this? I can't become a Forgotten. There's no one else to take care of my parents.*

Reaching her desk, Dez couldn't help but feel as if all the surveillance cameras pointed straight at her.

Just as in Euporia, Animus's historically bright skies had faded, and the air was cool. If evil continued to grow in the planes, the land would soon be in perpetual darkness. Lumen were strategically placed throughout the tumultuous world in order to keep the Murk from the loci leading to the planes. They were successful thus far, but Animus was crawling with Murk. Any more ambushes by the enemy and the planes would be vulnerable. With fewer guards and a thinning atmosphere, the Murk might be able to finally reach people.

6

● ● ●

ARABELLA QUICKLY MADE her way down the steep stone stairs. Reaching the bottom, she slid her hand across the cool wall until she found the light switch. With a flick of her finger, the basement lights began to steadily awake. Arabella was the only person to ever visit the lowest level of the house, except for the security detail on their daily sweep of the entire property. Maximillian was afraid of the cold undecorated space, and Benjamina was uninterested in reliving the past.

The basement was practically empty except for a small pile of boxes filled with Caius's former belongings. The boxes of keepsakes were stacked inside an arched cutout under the stairs of the cavernous room. The blank white walls of the basement reflected the bright fluorescent lights, which created a blinding glow. The room stretched the entire footprint of the mansion. The silence was unnerving.

While Arabella had never skipped school to reminisce, she rushed over to the familiar boxes that she regularly explored in her free time. These frequent journeys kept the memories of her father fresh. She had a routine to sort through her father's last possessions. She carefully placed the contents of the five boxes across the gray lacquered floor.

Box one contained Caius's remaining clothes. There were only a few garments in the box, and they were much more casual than expected for the spouse of an Aurelian official. Arabella relished pulling Caius's favorite T-shirt over her clothes and breathing in her father's fading timbered scent. The fourteen-year-old hastily jerked the pitch-black shirt over her head. On the front bottom left hem was stitched in gray cursive font: *Vultus.*

Once she donned his shirt, Arabella moved on to boxes two and three, Caius's crimson-red hardcover journals. She enjoyed randomly leafing through his recollections. Arabella would select one entry to read each visit to the basement. She commonly found that Maximillian and herself were the subjects of his writings. Today, *Journal 15*, the last in the collection, caught her eye. Gingerly, she opened to August 8, Caius's final entry, a note she avoided until today.

August 8:

Today, I went to Gryffin Park with Arabella and Maximillian. It is our favorite park because of the expansive woods and beautiful ponds. There is so much wildlife to sketch, and there is a magical quality about this place. While Maximillian chased Arabella with a slimy rana, I took a moment today to draw the landscape. I'm excited to frame this sketch for my little Arabella's 10th birthday!

We still don't have any concrete plans for my princess's birthday. Benjamina is too busy, as always, to take time to address our children's lives. I know she is important to Aurelia, but we're important too. Maybe one day she will understand. Ever since she won her election as the National Financier, we have continued to grow apart. She will never step down from her post, so I do not see things improving any time soon.

Well, she is calling for me now. I must be needed for a photo op. I'll have to finish this entry tomorrow.

Even though Arabella was saddened by this revelation about the state of her parents' marriage, she kept moving through the boxes. She had to hurry; her mother and music teacher would find her soon enough. There was no time for her to unpack all this emotional baggage.

Arabella opened boxes four and five, which held photo albums and sketches. She saved her favorite boxes for last. Even though it was becoming more difficult every day to remember the specifics of her father's face, she never wanted to forget his appearance. The photographs were her lifeline to remember her handsome dad. Caius was the only one in the family to have sandy-brown hair, green eyes, and stand above five-foot-nine.

Arabella preferred to look through pictures of her intact family. Today, however, she did not want to be reminded of her family's turbulence. The girl's deflection led her to an album she rarely cracked open, entitled *Friends*. Next to each picture was a description in the margin of the subjects in the photo.

Three-quarters of the way through the album, Arabella found a picture that she previously neglected. This time, her eyes were immediately drawn to a photo of her mother, father, and an odd-looking friend. She looked to the margin and could find no name for the acquaintance. Caius was the only one smiling in the picture, while Benjamina frowned, and the other looked off in the distance to an unknown subject.

Taking a moment to scrutinize the photo further, Arabella realized there was something strangely familiar about the third character. She was almost certain they appeared in one of her many reoccurring dreams. While sleeping, Arabella frequently experienced short flickers of a scene where this individual stood before her. Each time, she could sense other people around her in the dream, but like a magnet, her eyes were fixed on the mysterious stranger. The engrossed teen could never discern the words spoken but always tried.

Suddenly, Arabella recognized the clicking of heeled staccato footsteps growing louder near the basement door. The pace was unmistakable; Benjamina was coming. With one hand, Arabella fearfully threw off her father's T-shirt and, with the other hand, ripped the newly discovered picture from its space. As she stuffed the snapshot in her dress pocket, she noticed writing on the back of the photo that looked like prose. Arabella ran toward the stairs, leaving the array of mementos strewn on the floor; she would come back tonight to organize her treasures. As Benjamina's face appeared within the doorframe, Arabella met her at the top step.

The omniscient Author's poem was unfolding. Lumen were poised for battle, and the three heroes were developing their roles in the story. Author sprung from Animus to Euporia in anticipation of a divine encounter. Author appeared on a private elevator face-to-face with Mr. Rothchild, whose appearance assaulted the senses. In his second outfit of the day, Mr. Rothchild was dressed in an electric-blue and neon-green plaid suit and doused in a bucket of musky cologne. "Good afternoon, Switcher," Author said too cheerily based on the two's contentious and lengthy history.

"What are you so happy about? My Murk are multiplying faster than ever because of people's evil acts, and your Lumen are outmatched due to people's neglect for good acts," the Switcher stated emphatically with a glint in its eyes.

Author rebuffed the ostentatious Switcher. "You have no idea what's been set in motion, but you inevitably will. You do not know people like I do, and because of your lack of perception, you will most assuredly lose in the end."

The Switcher arrogantly laughed and quickly brushed aside Author's warning. "I've won so far. In your absence, we have thrived. Resentment grows in silence. People do not know you anymore, and if they do, they do not consider you. You're in denial that your ink is still flowing, but I am bringing your book to a frightening close."

Completely unaffected, Author calmly said, "You are a fool to think I have been silent. This volume will soon conclude, but there will be another, and it will have no end. I have already started this next work of art because I love them. I love them much more than you hate them. Switcher, I will see you again soon in one plane or another, and in one form or another."

"Floor one hundred. Welcome Mr. Rothchild," a voice sunnily chimed over the intercom of the elevator. Without looking back and without a parting farewell, the Switcher walked out of the elevator into its extravagant office. Author pressed 1 as the elevator doors slid closed.

7

AURELIA MONDAY 1:27 P.M.

"WHAT ARE YOU doing down there? Why are you not in music class with your brother? He said you were sick, but you look fine to me," Benjamina demanded with an angry glare. With the photograph burning a hole in her dress pocket, Arabella answered, "I miss Dad." The innocent child stared at her feet while her mother stood in intimidating silence.

Arabella caved under Benjamina's pressure and spoke fast, very fast. "Mom, I'm so sorry for skipping class. It's just, I started to practice 'A Daughter's Dance.' And, I started to miss Dad. And, I just had to go through his things. And, I was going through his journals . . ."

Benjamina looked through her daughter and answered with little emotion. "Arabella, you are too old for this. It has been four years. You need to move on now! I don't have time for this. I certainly don't have time to talk about the past. You need to focus on your future. It's time to go to math and then science. I'm going to walk you to class. Don't let me catch you down there again."

Arabella practically ran next to her mother as they made their way through the winding corridors of the vast mansion. The hallways were lined with priceless fine art: statues, busts, ceramics, paintings, and most importantly, the official portraits of family members who served as national financier. They approached a mini amphitheater filled with wall-to-wall digital screens, built only for the Rey children. Benjamina came to a sudden stop and breathed deep her lavender fragrance. Both parties hoped the scent would calm the irritated adult quickly.

The mother looked her daughter square in the eyes, now with some compassion, and said, "This family is important in Aurelia, and Aurelia needs you to succeed. Your success starts in the classroom. Focus so that one day you can become national financier too. You must look forward, not back." Without hesitation or any show of affection, Benjamina promptly walked away from her daughter.

Arabella was present physically for math with Mrs. Diaz and science with Mr. Abdallah but not mentally. She couldn't shake her mother's words. The guilt and shame of disappointing her only living parent were a familiar product of conversations with Benjamina. She was still not used to her mother's soapbox of perfectionism, or the apathy toward her father's death. Arabella wondered how her mother could get passed her father's tragic and unexpected death so quickly. The nation of Aurelia seemed to mourn longer than Benjamina.

Arabella was startled from her thoughts as Maximillian gave her a gentle shove from the seat behind. "What's wrong with you? You skipped out on music class, and you didn't answer a single question all afternoon. Am I finally starting to rub off on you?"

Still preoccupied, Arabella asked, "Do you ever remember seeing them?" Looking around for any eavesdroppers, Arabella slowly slid the newly unearthed photograph from her fashionable dress and pointed to the stranger.

Maximillian snatched the picture and studied it closely. "Who's that?"

Arabella seized the snapshot back. "So, you don't recognize them either?"

"Nope, but I recognize the park. That's Gryffin Park," he stated, pleased with his discovery.

Arabella was so perplexed by the subject of the photo that she totally missed the backdrop of the image. "Oh, my gosh! Of course, that *is* Gryffin Park." The siblings strolled toward the exit of the high-tech science lab. They passed the still-warm burners and half-full bubbling beakers. All the while, Arabella was methodically mapping the quickest route to the beloved park in her mind.

As they reached the domed atrium in the center of the home, Maximillian split from his sister toward his room on the west wing. Arabella gave a small wave to her energetic brother as he bound down his hallway. Instead of heading down her hallway toward her bedroom in the east wing, she crept toward the front door. She needed to go investigate the location of the curious photograph. If her mother wouldn't give her answers, could she find them for herself even after all these years? Unsure of what she was even looking for, Arabella decided to leave the premises without her personal escort.

The inexperienced sleuth edged along the exterior stone walls of the manor to avoid the outward facing security cameras. This was her first time sneaking off the family property, but she and Maximillian had played hide-and-go-seek with the idle security detail enough times to know how to stay hidden from the dozens of cameras lining the roof of the home.

Really, the game was actually "hide-and-go-undetected" with the security guards. The ten rotating guards who manned the in-home security suite watched for glimpses of the children on the monitors. If one of them was spotted on a screen, the identifying guard would gaily announce the child's location over the intercom system.

By and large, the security team, led by Frank Rusco, was friendly to the children. Arabella wondered if the employees were kind to her out of duty or true fondness. Frank was a towering man, at six-foot-three, retired from the Aurelian military. He appeared to be in his late thirties, but was in his mid-forties. The imposing man was bald, brown-eyed, and sported a dark-brown trimmed beard. Every day, as team leader, Frank wore a fitted navy sport jacket and a clear earpiece in his left ear.

Arabella was closest with Frank out of all the security team, and Frank seemed particularly attached to Arabella and Maximillian.

For years, he would slip Arabella and her brother dulcis bread, their favorite pastry. Benjamina only allowed dulcis bread on holidays because it was so sweet, so the children quickly devoured the culinary contraband.

Arabella reached the back corner of the stone edifice, where a large fruit tree grew. This favorite hiding spot kept her undetectable and had an endless supply of gavy fruit, an Aurelian delicacy. The bark of the trunk and branches of the tree were a navy hue, while the fist-sized fruits were vibrant gold. Arabella loved the sour taste of the odd plant.

The agile teenager sprinted to the trunk of the tree and, in a leap, landed on the lowest branch. She climbed another ten feet before she balanced along a limb that extended across the high stone barrier. Arabella shimmied along the offshoot until she hovered above the sidewalk below. Slowly lowering herself, she hung below the sturdy branch with her hands high above her head. Without a second thought, the teen girl dropped to the unconfined domain.

As fast as Arabella's legs could carry her, she ran the mile to Gryffin Park's entrance. After Caius's death, which went unexplained, Benjamina restricted the children's play to the expansive family property. The fear of another death within the family meant Arabella and Maximillian had not left the premises without a strong security presence in four years. Parks were not among the approved locations listed for the children to travel.

Taking a moment to breathe in her freedom, Arabella observed the dense woods and large ponds. They were exactly as she remembered. She withdrew the now bent photograph and searched for the location where the picture was originally taken. Holding the picture at arm's length in front of her, Arabella meandered through the landscape, looking for a matching feature. Finally, she reached a distinctive tree; it had one stump but grew three intertwined trunks. This tree was undeniably the same tree in the snapshot taken years ago.

Arabella roamed around the tree's massive trunk looking for any clues that might stir her memory. After a few minutes of walking in circles and no luck, she slumped against the base of the tree. Tilting her head back in frustration, Arabella was ready to quit and go home. Suddenly, in her periphery, she glimpsed an obscure light. Her head twisted to the right to get a better look at the source of the illumination. One single braided rope of beams was almost touching Arabella's nose. She reached for the luminescent cord. As Arabella looked closer, she realized this one strand was the last in a long line as far as her eye could see. She effortlessly pushed the fringe of light to the side and, with it, her reality.

Mr. Rothchild rose from his ornate ivory desk and walked through the impossibly large glass doors to the helipad. At a quick pace, he crossed the rooftop to the edge of the 100th floor. Without hesitation, Mr. Rothchild stepped off the edge of the building and disappeared into thin air.

The Switcher emerged from Euporia into Animus, where battalions of reinforcement Murk awaited orders. The tall, emaciated, and shadowy creature proudly stated to its underlings, "Victory is assured. I have waited millennia for this opportunity. I was there in the beginning, and I sowed the first seeds of wickedness. People have finally perpetrated enough evil that we are at our pinnacle." The rank-and-file Murk hissed in approval.

The ghastly figure continued, "It was their wrongdoing that split their world apart into three planes. Long ago, families and friends were separated, and now they are none the wiser. It was my plan all along to weaken their bonds. That fool, Author, allowed the world to be fractured. Little did Author know, I'd use this divide against that naïf to destroy humanity." The caliginous Murk swayed with fervor.

The giant eye of a storm formed above the Switcher's head. "In the near future, we will have visitors. Let's make sure to give them a cold welcome."

8

WALTER SPRINTED BACK to the charging center to find his friends anxiously waiting for him.

"There he is!" Pete yelled, relieved.

"Get in the car. We're late!" Brian exclaimed, exasperated, as he started the motor. Brian hoped to remain at the top of their class, and arriving late on the first day of school was no way to achieve his goal.

Walter dove into the front passenger seat while Pete swatted the top of his head over the headrest. "Don't get me wrong. I don't mind missing Mrs. Anderson's math class, but even I try not to be late on the first day of school. I'm going to VEX that I'm already putting my books in my locker, and hopefully my mom will fall for it. Maybe she'll be too busy at work to check my geotag," Pete schemed to avoid a grounding from his single-parent mother, Patricia. Most of the time, she was occupied with her Fizz shop.

Fizz was the most VEX'd about drink in Immerxia. The consumer mixed unflavored packets of Vervate, the highest legal dose of caffeine, with the drink of their choice. An instantaneous burst of carbon dioxide was released when the powder touched the liquid, which created the reaction the namesake was famous for. The people of Immerxia drank about five cups a day.

Brian floored the pedal across town to CommX Academy. He hoped the Immerxia Police Department was too preoccupied sharing

VEXs about their most up-to-date equipment to patrol for speeding teens. Reaching school, Brian parked in the back of the overflow parking lot, and the three students hurried up to the lusterless school entrance. The academic building was cement and asymmetrical. There was very little green space and no welcoming features. Whoever built the school did not care to design an inviting academy.

The unpunctual teens ran through the deserted hallways to their first-period class. No school officials even noticed that the three boys were fifteen minutes tardy on the first day. Everyone, faculty and students, were already in their respective rooms on their electronic devices. Brian bravely entered the classroom leading his friends, but no one even looked up.

At the front of the classroom, Mrs. Anderson, an uninspiring woman, was reclined with her feet on the desk. She was busy taking screenshots of the advanced calculators she planned to peddle to her mathematics students in hopes of making some extra money. Her prerecorded welcome video played on the projector screen. The animated Mrs. Anderson in the projection did not match the apathetic woman sitting at the front of the room. The students were fixated on their personal devices and were more likely to see their teacher on their screens than in real life.

As Walter took the last open seat in the back corner next to his introverted classmate, Caroline Moore, it was not lost on him how impersonal his junior year began. Unlike most of his peers, Walter tried to pay attention to the introduction to junior math, but Author's words continued to swirl around in his head.

The best part of the class came when Stacey looked over her shoulder and mouthed, "I'm sorry. He just sat down," discreetly pointing to the popular and ridiculously handsome Jeff Miller sitting next to her. All Walter could muster was a nervous wave and a goofy grin.

After what felt like an eternity, Walter stepped out of the classroom and searched the hallway for his love interest. He spotted Stacey's stunning blue-black, wavy ponytail, that contrasted perfectly against her caramel skin. To his surprise, especially since the students only had five minutes between first and second period, she was lingering right outside the classroom door. Brian and Pete were nowhere to be found and must have already moved on to their next class.

"Way to be late on the first day of school," Stacey flirtatiously joked.

"It's a long story. I'll have to tell you over lunch?" he posited as more of a question than a statement.

"I can't wait to hear about it, Wally. I'll definitely save you a seat," Stacey said as she walked away from the charmed boy toward her next class.

He stood stunned for a few seconds, dazed by her lingering floral perfume. Suddenly, he realized there were only three minutes to reach gym class on the other side of the school. The cement building was as big as it was lackluster. As he jogged across campus, he couldn't help but smile at his nearing lunch date with his perfectly polished crush. The anticipation of the date was just what he needed to distract him from the questions still looming after his brush with Author.

Walter was glad to have gym for second period with Pete. Everyone knew physical education was the favorite class in school, especially since there was no teacher present. Instead of an instructor, their smart shoes logged the students' physical activity, everything from running to bowling. Also, it was required of all juniors to use their smart devices to VEX at least once every fifteen minutes of the ninety minutes to try to offset costs of the academy's technology department. Grades were based on a combination of the amount of physical energy exerted and how much money each student was able to generate. Walter possessed a false sense of hope that he would finally achieve higher than a C on his usually mediocre report card.

"Pete, you'll never guess who I'm eating lunch with today," Walter enthusiastically stated as the friends slowly stretched their arms across their bodies.

"I didn't know your mom was coming to the school for lunch," Pete quipped.

"No, you jerk! Stacey said she'd save me a seat at lunch," Walter shot back.

"Like she saved you a seat in math?" Pete sarcastically questioned.

"She tried to save me a seat, but stupid Jeff sat down first. She's going to save me a seat at lunch. I know it. This is the year, Pete. I'm finally going to ask her out," Walter stated with a hint of confidence.

"You know you're not the only one who is interested in Stacey. Brian and half the other boys in our class want to date her," Pete said with very little hope for Walter's chances.

"Well, she didn't wait for any other guy after first period. Did she? This is my year," Walter said, concluding his case.

Before Pete could ask about the events of Walter's disappearance this morning or give him a harder time about his crush, Walter slipped away from his friend, knowing he would continue to stretch and VEX for the full ninety minutes instead of breaking a sweat. Pete's strategy was to avoid working out by raising money for the school.

Walter jogged over to a group of familiar students preparing to play a game of Bounce, a competition created by the students to exert the most energy in the shortest amount of time. Bounce was a battle royale ball game on indoor trampolines, and it was the most popular sport among the unsupervised adolescents. It could become quite wild without an adult present and commonly ended with multiple students receiving minor injuries. The focus on technology kept the faculty and staff from noticing or intervening in the raucous activity.

After taking a ball to the face, Walter was eliminated about halfway through the game, which was better than he usually performed. He attributed his marginal improvement to the positive interaction with Stacey that morning. Walter stood on the sideline VEXing as each successive player was pummeled.

In the smelly locker room, Walter made sure to spritz himself a couple extra times with his pungent body spray and applied a couple extra layers of deodorant. In his excitement, he neglected to wait for Pete before leaving the suffocating area. Walter practically sprinted down the hall to the cafeteria to save Stacey a seat and avoid a repeat of this morning.

Walter approached Vigo's Casseroles, a frequent spot for him in the school food court. He VEX'd about the inexpensive casseroles so much that he was able to gain enough food credit to receive free lunch. Very few of Walter's cohort advertised Vigo's meals, even though the casseroles were quite good. Walter's primary audience was the forty-and-above crowd who frequented Vigo's main restaurant downtown.

Vigo greeted Walter with his usual gruff tone. "Here. Veggie casserole." Walter accepted his least favorite casserole without batting an eye. He was too focused on snagging two seats together.

Just as Walter sat in the almost empty cafeteria, Stacey entered through the double doors and instantly waved at Walter. She excitedly projected, "Let me get my food. I'll be right there." Stacey went straight to the counter at Em's Pokits. She used food credits to purchase her favorite, the sweet pokit, at the popular and expensive eatery. Stacey had VEXing down to a science; she was even better than Brian. No junior had stockpiled as many food credits as Stacey. Walter, along with the rest of the student body, waited in anticipation for all of Stacey's VEXs, even about the unremarkable entrées.

Stacey gracefully walked up to Walter, and as she sat, her hand rested on his shoulder. "I've been dying to hear your story about this morning. Tell me everything."

Walter made sure to skip the morning's events highlighting Brian, especially his new car. He began with zest. "I haven't told anyone about this yet. You have to promise to keep this between us. You're not going to believe what I saw this morning. I don't know if I even believe what I saw this morning."

Stacey was on the edge of her seat. "Oh, my goodness. Tell me. I have to know."

He continued, "I saw something. It was like a ghost. It's almost like it wasn't real, but I was led to—"

The boisterous Jeff interrupted. "Hey, Stacey! I've been looking for you. I didn't get to finish telling you about my summer this morning."

Both Walter and Stacey were caught off guard by a group of popular students approaching their table: Jeff Miller, Carrie Harris, Donovan Parker, and Maya Hernandez. Jeff sat across from Stacey, hoping to steal her attention away from Walter. All the newcomers were acquaintances of Walter but friends of Stacey. Walter suddenly felt unwelcome on his own lunch date. To his delight, Stacey seemed just as unhappy about the intrusion.

"You got the same pokit as me, Stacey," Jeff said, flirting awkwardly as he held up the oozing chocolate and vanilla pokit. The kids looked around the table as they evaluated each other's lunches. For a few minutes, the group discussed the merits of their meals, but Walter astutely perceived Carrie's silence. He looked across the table, and in front of Carrie sat a small brown bag lunch. She quickly ate the miniscule meal consisting of a dried fruit and a small bag of plain crispy wafers as the students discussed their most popular VEXs of the summer.

The noticeably thin Carrie reluctantly handed Walter her empty brown bag. "Can you toss this in the trash? The can is just behind you."

Walter quickly responded out of sympathy. "Of course." With an outstretched hand, he kindly accepted the crumpled bag. Walter stood to walk to the bin, but as he was turning, he felt the weight of the used sack significantly increase. "Oh . . . there's something in here," Walter stated as he spun back around. Carrie skeptically retrieved the mysterious bag, wondering if this was a cruel ruse.

The doubtful girl peeked inside and froze. She looked up at Walter with wide eyes and said, "How did you do that?"

"Do what?" Walter quizzically responded.

Carrie looked to see if the other peers were listening, but no one appeared to be paying attention. She whispered, "There was nothing in the bag when I handed it to you, but now there's—" The bell rudely interrupted, signaling the end of the lunch period.

Out of gratitude, Carrie rounded the table and quickly embraced Walter. She whispered in his ear, "Thank you," and walked away from the befuddled boy. Walter continued to watch Carrie as she moved toward the exit and lifted a massive meat pokit from the brown receptacle. With a large smile, she began to eat the coveted entree.

Walter's CommX8 buzzed. He glanced at his communication device and saw the name Author (whose name Walter had not added to his contacts). *"You just made Carrie's day. You know where to find me,"* Walter read to himself as his jaw dropped.

Stacey broke Walter from his daze. "Sorry my friends interrupted our conversation. Want to talk after school? I'm determined to hear your mind-blowing story."

Walter couldn't believe it, but he was going to turn down a proper date with his long-standing crush. "I really want to, but I have something I have to do after school today. Can we meet tomorrow?"

Clearly disappointed, Stacey replied, "I guess I can wait. It's a date. We can walk to Pat's Fizz Shop after school."

Walter enthusiastically accepted her invitation but wondered if a conversation with the puzzling Author was worth missing a date with Stacey. He also worried that the next twenty-four hours would afford another admirer to make an advance at Stacey. The pair reluctantly parted for their afternoon courses. Walter spent the afternoon recounting all the odd events from the day and awaited answers from Author.

Two bright, ethereal beings approached each other away from the waging war. One was Selfless and one was Virtue. Their language was music notes because they could not speak words. The melodic conversation began. Virtue played first. "Welcome, Selfless. We're so glad you were created. It's rare we get reinforcements these days, particularly your kind. What questions do you have?"

Selfless played next. "I know much about myself, like I was born from a selfless act by an Immerxian. But tell me, what is required of me now? It's much darker here than I expected. Where are the rest of the Lumen?"

The song continued by Virtue, "It is increasingly dark here. All existing Lumen are either battling the Murk or guarding the loci. I was sent to retrieve you and take you to the frontline with me. You are much needed here."

The beautiful tune persevered as Virtue and Selfless whisked toward battle.

9

EUPORIA MONDAY 8:02 P.M.

IT WAS JUST after eight o'clock, and floor thirty-three was unnervingly empty. Dez was in absolute darkness except for the glow from her computer. She thought to herself, *E-Corp is so cheap. Why can't they just pay for the lights to stay on if someone's on the floor?* The small light illuminated only Dez's cubicle, and it was the only thing to give her a sense of safety. Just moments ago, all the employees on the floor retreated to their paltry apartments after a grueling day of work. Even after her encounter with Val, Dez was still hard at work, knowing she must do anything to secure her job so that she could take care of her parents. This meant working overtime, except without extra pay.

The night shift started their stint at nine o'clock, so Dez had an hour to accomplish as much coding as possible. To help keep the nocturnal workers "motivated," they were granted one less hour of work per day compared to the day shift. Management's tactics did nothing to improve the productivity numbers of the graveyard shift, though, as their numbers were consistently lower than the day team's.

Dez's exhausted fingers typed fiercely, but her mind waned as she grew increasingly fatigued. Twelve-hour workdays were demanding at best, and deliberately punishing at worst. To add on an extra hour was madness. Dez knew that many more such workdays were in her future if she wanted to maintain her family's meager lifestyle; the alternative was to become Forgotten.

The Vac-Trition coding she had done now felt like ages ago, but in reality, Dez submitted those projects just a few hours earlier. She was now coding the soon-to-be mandatory E-Watch. This accessory was not much of a watch, though. It was designed to track the employees' whereabouts, hours, and productivity while in any E-Corp facility. Rumor had it that the E-Watch would track the wearers outside of official buildings as well.

Employees could only use the device for telling time when they were at home, since E-Corp believed telling time was only necessary to arrive promptly at work. Once in the building, E-Corp believed there was no need to watch the clock and dream for the end of the workday. This was a distraction. E-Corp would keep the time for everyone.

Dez hoped by coding this product ahead of schedule, she could grab the attention of Management—in a good way this time. This project was not slated for coding until next week. While she wasn't trying to become employee of the month, Dez knew she was in Ms. Mayflower's sights. This project was a top-tier priority for the CEO, Mr. Rothchild. If he was happy, all of Management was happy.

Even though Dez dreaded wearing the new wrist tracker, she made excellent progress on her first day of coding this surveilling invention. She pressed the save button located in the center of the keyboard. All computers on the E-Corp property automatically saved work every fifteen minutes, but Dez didn't want to take any chances.

Suddenly, the program shrunk in on itself as if the words and images were being sucked back deep into the computer. Within seconds, the entire screen was as dark as the furthest corner of floor thirty-three. The keyboard was the only thing in the room with any sign of life, even more life than Dez, whose heart had momentarily stopped beating.

Her first exhale was accompanied by a stifled scream that reverberated around the empty floor, quickly followed by, "Crap! The nightly reboot. I totally forgot." Every night, E-Corp shut down all company computers to scan for personal folders. Not only did the conglomerate scan and remove personal files, but they also uploaded company data. These programs were anything designed to increase profits for the managers.

Dez hammered the power button with her right index finger, but users retained no control over their workstation when the reboot started. She sat powerless for what felt like a lifetime but was actually only a few minutes. As the computer began to slowly brighten and change colors, finally the login screen appeared.

Dez hastily lined her fingertips up with the corresponding keys. A warning flashed on the screen, *USER NOT RECOGNIZED!* She looked down and realized her hands and arms were dripping with sweat. Dez hurriedly wiped her hands on her uniform pants. She then used the worn sleeve of her uniform to wipe dry the flat keys.

The home screen appeared after another attempt by Dez to login. She started to tap her finger on the E-Corp icon in the top left corner of the otherwise empty touchscreen. She paused. A new icon in the middle of the display caught her attention. It was in the shape of an open book. Dez was even more intrigued by the new program since it shared her first name, Destiny. *This must be a new program just installed by E-Corp,* Dez thought.

She opened the file, and a lone window popped up with what appeared to be a short poem. Dez considered not reading the prose but persisted because nothing was ever accidentally uploaded on company drives.

Three planes from one

Due to evil that was done

Animus holds Lumen and Murk

Here Switcher comes and goes to lurk

One hero from each plane

To bring healing of all pain

Past, present, future altered with gifts

Join together to mend rifts

Switcher will see defeat

Only then will restoration be complete.

Bewildered, Dez tilted her head in hopes that the words would make more sense sideways. They didn't. She read the poem two more times. Neither the piece nor the program exhibited an identifiable author. This was almost more baffling than the words of the poem; E-Corp ensured all work products were traceable to individual employees. Dez began to believe she stumbled upon an unsanctioned file. She thought about reporting this unknown program to her manager but was certain she would be blamed for the illicit material. With three minutes left until the next shift entered the floor, Dez grabbed a marker off her desk and scribbled the short poem messily down the length of her arm in the dim light.

Moments later, an elevator dinged on the thirty-third floor, signaling the arrival of the night shift. Almost simultaneously, the bright industrial lights burst to life. In a panic, Dez found the options section of the program and selected *DELETE.* She did not want the next occupant of her station to find the damning file. It was uncommon for employees to delete anything off their station computers, so the action required fingerprint verification. Her manager would soon be notified that something was erased, and E-Corp would quickly know the contents of the program that she deleted. The elevator doors opened, and silent people began to flood onto the now bright floor.

Dez seized her few belongings and jumped out from her cubicle as her vision adjusted to the assault of light. The dispirited serfs of the next shift were not paying attention, but if they were, all that was visible of Dez was her brown hair flying through the emergency exit toward the stairwell. With a rush of adrenaline, Dez ran down all thirty-three flights of stairs. She sailed through the building's lobby undetected and out the front door into the cool night.

The moon was as rare to see in Euporia as the sun, and tonight was no exception, but Dez stopped and looked up at the dark sky anyway. This reprieve was short-lived as the reality of her problematic situation set in. Dez thought, *How am I going to avoid retribution from Ms. Mayflower for deleting a program? I've already received one warning. I don't think I'll get another.*

Author was satisfied with Dez's discovery and knew the others would soon share in this revelation. While standing on a favorite hilltop in Animus, the powerful being surveyed the planes. Like magnets, the Lumen were drawn to their leader and assembled. Author proudly stated, "It's time." In one accord, the purveyors of light nodded their heads and prepared for the looming final battle.

10

ANIMUS MONDAY 5:37 P.M.

● ● ●

THE WORLD WAS full of dimming light, odd vegetation, and rolling plains. In Animus, an expansive ethereal sky twinkled as if at twilight. The gentle hills were covered in knee-high vegetation. The otherworldly plants, from stems to petals, were lined with beads of light that flickered like fireflies. The blooms of the plants faintly glowed a stunning yellow, only comparable to the color of the sun. Humans and their development did not exist in this world.

This place was as fierce as it was beautiful. In stark contrast to this unnatural beauty, Lumen and Murk violently clashed continuously in battle across the sprawling landscape. On the horizon, sparks of light and thunderous commotion developed among the skirmishes. The storms could be heard all around before they were seen.

As Arabella's eyes adjusted to the duskiness of the alien world, she felt uneasy in her solitude. Suddenly, a clap of thunder seized her attention. She looked in the direction of the reverberating noise. Along with the tumult was a clash of the outlines of light and dark beings. The shadowy figures were twice as large as the opposing entities. To Arabella, the creatures, both Lumen and Murk, bore only the faintest resemblance to humans. They all appeared blurry or out of focus to the teenage girl. She did not know if this was from their fast movements, their distance away, or if this was their natural state.

The girl crouched to hide among the crawling flora. She parted the plants to continue to observe this unconventional fight. The sight was so surreal that Arabella wondered if this was all a figment of her imagination. Was this all just a dream? Would she soon wake up in Gryffin Park?

An obviously large shadow appeared at the front of the two warring groups, and an exceptionally bright light stood in its path, protecting the dimmer illuminations behind. For a few minutes, the two most powerful warriors among the Lumen and Murk traded blows of contrasting hues. The two beings manipulated the light and darkness to form projectiles with their phantom extremities. The darker tones hit the Lumen with precision while the brighter tones were harmlessly deflected off their mark.

The dark challenger advanced closer. The size difference between the two combatants became even more apparent. Sensing a victory was near, the supporting Murk rumbled as if forming an earthquake. Fearing another defeat, the Lumen began to back away from their leader, taking their dim light with them.

A rushing sound emanated from the forceful Murk, and the brilliant Lumen was pulled in the direction of the dark form. The Lumen dug into the vegetation below. As if hoping to help, the plants tried to wrap around the lower half of the virtuous phantom. Within the blink of an eye and an agonizing low note of despair, the Lumen was engulfed into the victorious Murk. The champion was unscathed and appeared to emerge stronger; the creature incorporated the power of the defeated Lumen into its essence. The remaining leaders of the small company of Lumen sounded a brassy retreat so as not to be consumed as well. The withdrawal left the Murk alone on the battlefield, emanating a deep and taunting reverberation.

The terrified and misplaced teen did not know what the dark creatures would do to her if captured, but she knew she did not stand a chance of surviving. Still in a squat, Arabella spun around, looking to escape the suddenly treacherous place. A confusing scene lay before Arabella. On the other side of the locus that she previously entered through, there stood an array of buildings, people, vehicles, and terrains. Three distinctive worlds seemed to overlap. Arabella was able to distinguish Gryffin Park, but also found a looming skyscraper and a small suburban house lying among her beloved trees.

A teenage boy climbing stairs suspended in midair came into Arabella's view. She discreetly waved her arms to hopefully gain his attention and aid. He continued climbing to the left of Arabella without even a glance in her direction.

Within a second, a high-end chrome car appeared to her right, traveling at a very high speed in the direction of the boy. Impossibly, it looked as if the car was in line to strike the teenager on the hovering stairs. Arabella's instinct to help surged as she jumped from her hunched position and sprinted toward the adolescent. Not knowing what else to do, she lunged toward the locus and through the atmosphere.

Arabella sailed through the air with her arms outstretched, hoping to push the boy out of danger. To her surprise, the only thing she felt was her hands hitting the pavement. No boy. No stairs.

Brakes screeched as the reflective automobile nearly missed Arabella. The vehicle came to an abrupt halt, and the driver's door swung open. As she lay dazed on the road, the driver yelled, "What are you doing? You could have ruined my car. You're so—"

The man paused when he noticed the girl's lack of uniform but expensive attire. "What are you doing down here? You're not Tech. I'm heading to the ninety-second floor of Management quarters. Do you need help finding your way back? I'm sure your parents don't want a girl like you down here." Arabella stared blankly up at the stranger.

"What happened to the boy? Did you hit him?" she asked frantically.

The well-dressed executive in a tailored blue suit chuckled. "The only person in the road was you. Are you alright? What division do your parents manage? I'll help you get back to them."

Slightly scraped up, Arabella responded with pride, "I'm fine. My mom is the national financier. I just need you to point me toward Golden Ray Avenue."

"Golden Ray Avenue? There are no roads by that name here. And there is no such job as national financier. Are you sure you're alright?" asked the rushed executive.

After a moment of calculation, Arabella sprung up from the asphalt and darted away from the unknown adult and toward the array of skyscrapers. The manager looked on with confusion but did not follow her.

Nothing looked familiar, but Arabella did not slow her pace. As she zoomed down the foreign streets, multitudes of people in white uniforms stared at her strangely. It was nighttime, and the street was mainly lit by the muted lights inside the office buildings. Helicopter blades chopping overhead broke the silence of the placid people.

After sprinting for what felt like a marathon, Arabella abruptly stopped. She looked around at the empty street. *Where is everyone?* Unsure of what to do next, she slipped into a small, unappealing café wedged between two skyscrapers. Just as outside, there were no people inside either. The restaurant consisted of a handful of tables, each with a single chair and a small light, and two six-foot tall machines to dole out meals. Arabella read the word *Vac-Trition* at the top of each contraption. The foreigner had never tasted a Vac-Trition meal before, but judging by the pictures, she wasn't about to, either. Everything Arabella observed suggested that the café was not for enjoyment but rather for necessity only.

The lost girl tiptoed to the table farthest from the street and sat. She felt heavy in the chair from the events of the overwhelming day. From shock, Arabella remained motionless and thoughtless. Finally, she channeled the one person she believed could help her escape this situation, her mother. Benjamina's voice swirled in Arabella's head. *You have to be smart now. You're not hurt. Stay calm and think. You can leverage your way out of this; you've seen me do that many times.* Her mother's voice began to grow louder and faster.

Keep your emotions in check; you know you can be sensitive. Don't cry. Stay in well-lit areas. Try not to stand out. Don't look lost. Find the right person. Someone you can trust. The list continued. *Okay, you've waited long enough.* The voice, completely unignorable now, shouted. *It's time to move! Go!*

As if the words controlled her, Arabella jumped up. Heeding some of her mother's advice, but not all of it, she began to run. She flew through the café doors and out into the chilly night. The drop in temperature suggested that she had spent much more time in the restaurant than she thought. Sprinting again, Arabella felt renewed strength in her legs after giving them much-needed rest.

The Aurelian rounded a massive building and collided with a girl about her age standing on the sidewalk staring skyward. Arabella grabbed the other girl's arm to try to stabilize herself, but both girls ended up sprawled on the hard pavement. They groaned from the impact and sat up slowly. The two painstakingly stood and dusted themselves off.

Now eye to eye, Arabella examined the girl across from her and saw that the accident almost completely tore the baggy left sleeve from the skinny girl's uniform. She observed an odd marking under the tear. "I'm so sorry. I'm completely lost. Are you okay?"

The other girl seemed confused that Arabella was speaking to her and even looked around to see if she was addressing someone else. Not many spoke to each other on the streets of Euporia, especially people of different statuses.

Arabella continued, "Sorry I tore your sleeve. I must have grabbed it on the way down. If you want, my tailor can fix it for you. By the way, my name is Arabella."

Finally, the other teenager spoke as she adjusted her sleeve. "It's alright. This sleeve was already hanging on by a thread anyways. I can get it fixed. I'm Dez."

Leaving the recently won battle, Hatred rumbled to the Switcher. Much like the Lumen, the Murk did not speak words but rather communicated with the sounds of a tempest. "Today's battle was won. The Lumen retreated after I consumed Joy. They were weak, much weaker than last time. It is happening as you said, Great Destroyer."

The Switcher communicated back with a thunderous roll, "Well done. You proved your worth. Hatred has always been my favorite servant. I am particularly grateful for those who commit acts to create your kind. Hatred is the purest form of evil and multiplies the fastest."

"Overseer of Evil, I must report one more thing," the powerful Murk stormed. "There was a girl on the outskirts of battle. It has been years since we have seen a human in Animus. We spotted her just before she disappeared through the boundary. We do not know which plane she entered."

The Switcher cracked back, "Grab the other Hatred. We will find her."

11

EUPORIA MONDAY 9:06 P.M.

● ● ●

DESPITE ARABELLA'S DAUNTING situation, she maintained her Aurelian pleasantries. "It's a pleasure to meet you, Dez. If it's not too much of a bother, could you point me in the direction of Golden Ray Avenue? I'm completely lost, and nothing looks familiar."

Dez did not want to push this new and interesting acquaintance away, especially since it was the second such encounter of the day. The weary introvert responded as empathetically as she could muster after a long day of work. "I'm sorry you can't find your way. Euporia is an easy place to get lost, but I've never heard of Golden Ray Avenue. There's not much golden about this place."

Arabella nervously began to twist her hair. Suddenly, she had a bright idea. "Oh, maybe you could tell me where the National Financier's Office is. My mom is the head of the agency," she proudly stated.

"So, you mean she's in Management?" the blue-collar Dez apprehensively asked. "I don't think there's a national financier for E-Corp, though. I doubt Mr. Rothchild would ever allow anyone else to manage his money."

"What? What do you mean by Management? What is E-Corp? Who is Mr. Rothchild? Where are we?" Arabella was breathless.

Dez responded with a puzzled gaze. "I'll start with your easiest question. We're in Euporia."

"Euporia? I've never even heard of Euporia. I'm from Aurelia," Arabella said.

Arabella started to wonder if Maximillian was pulling one of his infamous pranks. This wouldn't be the first time she was duped by her little brother. Maybe Dez was just part of the torturous joke. "Did Maximillian put you up to this? This is elaborate even for him."

"I don't know any Maximillians. In fact, I really don't know many people by their names. I mainly know a few E-Corp identification numbers. And, believe me, I wish this was all a joke," Dez said dryly.

Cold reality struck Arabella; she was once again in an unknown and possibly dangerous land. As her thoughts raced, her mind instinctively went to the picture of her parents in her dress pocket. Searching for any sense of security, Arabella pulled the crinkled photograph into the cool night. She held the intimate piece of home up to eye level. After a moment of transportation back to Aurelia, Arabella broke back into her perceived nightmare and lowered the picture.

The characteristically pale Dez became ghostly white. "Wh . . . What does that say?" she stuttered as her right hand clasped her left elbow. Dez insisted, "Show me what's written on the back of that paper!"

"On the back of this?" Arabella questioned as she flipped the photograph over. For the first time, Arabella focused on the writing on the backside of her treasure. "I think it's a poem." She began to read the cursive handwriting.

> "Three planes from one
> Due to evil that was done
> Animus holds Lumen and Murk . . ."

In unison, Dez joined the reading.

> "Here Switcher comes and goes to lurk
> One hero from each plane

To bring healing of all pain
Past, present, future altered with gifts. . ."

As Dez's voice became louder, Arabella's softened. The Aurelian slowly looked up at the Euporian quizzically. Dez was no longer looking in Arabella's direction but instead reading the scribbled text down her bare left arm.

"Join together to mend rifts
Switcher will see defeat
Only then will restoration be complete."

The girls stared at each other in stunned silence. Arabella, being less reserved, spoke first. "Why is that on your arm? Are you sure you don't know my family? That's who's in this picture. And . . ."

Dez interrupted, "I found this poem on my work computer. It just happened to be there after the nightly reboot. Who's your family again?" Dez asked, hoping to theorize about their inexplicable connection.

"I'm part of the Rey family. You know, Benjamina Rey. Maximillian Rey. And me, Arabella Rey."

"I have no idea who you are talking about. I guess I should assume you scored Management on your PLACE exam. Have you heard anything about this poem being uploaded? Do you know what E-Corp plans to do with it?" Dez asked.

"I'm homeschooled and have never taken that test. Like I said, I just found this picture with the poem on the back in some family heirlooms today," Arabella answered.

Dez inquired, "How did you get here again? You running into me seems like more than a coincidence."

Feeling like an alien, Arabella struggled to explain how she arrived in front of Dez. "Well, I went to the park. I saw these . . . I'd guess you'd call them lights, and the next thing I knew, I was on what seemed like another planet. I saw some things I can't explain. Ended up jumping into your world, and then I ran until our collision stopped me."

Dez continued as she ushered Arabella to follow her. "Tell me more about your Aurelia and this world you can't explain. I think I know someone who can help get you home and give us some answers. Follow me to The Core."

Arabella didn't know what kind of establishment was open at this hour, or what The Core was. It seemed like her only option was to go along with this soft-spoken girl. Aware of the risks of following a stranger to an unknown place, she heard her mother's voice in her head. *"You are always safest at home with me. Don't wander off with anyone that I haven't thoroughly vetted."* She knew it was too late to heed her mother's pragmatic advice, so her pace did not slow as she asked, "Do you want to change out of your torn uniform first?"

Dez led Arabella down the dark street along the spiritless glass giants away from her scant apartment. "Don't worry, I can get it fixed in The Core too. Anything is possible there. And the best part about being underground . . . no Management. They are too disgusted by the Forgotten and would never demean themselves by going in the tunnels."

After walking about three blocks, Dez took a hard right down an alley toward a tunnel opening. The inconspicuous and dreary entrance was unmarked and grimy. By this hour, every Euporian was settled in their place, so the entryway was deserted but for the two kids.

Walking side by side, the two made their long descent down the tunnel's slope to The Core.

"Lux, you must follow them. Do not let them out of your sight. You will be their indelible guide," Author said. In front of Author was a modulating array of colors that changed to another vibrant hue with each movement. With understanding, Lux let off two quick flashes of brilliant white light before returning to its usual state of gentle waves of varying colors.

"You know the Euporians are too petrified to notice your presence, but make sure to conceal yourself until the right opportunity presents. By now, the girls will have found each other. There is still so much they must do, and they will undoubtedly need your protection. I need you to be my right-hand. Now go!" Author saw two more quick flashes of light as Lux passed through the atmosphere to Euporia.

12

WALTER'S FEET RELUCTANTLY carried him toward the Xitus Library as Stacey's words, *"It's a date,"* rang in his ears. For all the resistance that his mind created, there was a force that pressed him forward to answers. If not for all the odd occurrences of the day, Walter would never choose to set foot in the library again.

The teenager was lost in thought when Caroline Moore rolled out in front of him in her wheelchair from the Main Street Pharmacy. "I'm so sorry, sir!" she quickly apologized, not realizing it was one of her classmates. "Oh, it's just you," she quipped.

"Hey, Caroline," Walter said. She waved his greeting away as she rolled slowly beside him. After about twenty steps, breaking the awkward silence, Walter asked, "Where are you heading?"

"Where I go every day after school. To hang out with my friends," Caroline facetiously answered.

Walter gave her a sideways glance to try to gauge her seriousness. Not knowing how to read his female peer, he shared, "I'm heading to the library. Don't ask. It's a long story."

Caroline relented, "Really? I'm heading to the library too."

Walter stopped in front of Caroline. He briefly lost his train of thought as he scanned her black wheelchair covered from seat to handles in punk-rock band stickers. "Wait. Why are you going to the library?" He was sure he did not want anyone else present for his conversation with the mysterious Author.

"I was actually being a little serious about going to see my friends. The characters in books provide the best company. I go every day to hang out. I'm not really plugged into the technology culture. I prefer books to VEXs." As the teens approached the steps of the large brick building, the slight girl turned away from Walter toward a stained glass ramp that he had never noticed before.

Walter's curious mind buzzed with questions about Caroline's daily routine, but he surprised even himself when he asked the simple but obvious question, "What's it like?"

"What do you mean? Oh, you mean rolling in this awesome ride?" Caroline quipped.

As Walter felt embarrassed by his possibly off-putting question, Caroline continued, "Honestly, I've been in it for so long that it's almost a part of me now. I've made this chair reflective of me. I saw you staring at all my stickers. Do you like any of these bands?"

Caroline's normally hard exterior softened when realizing a peer was trying to connect with her. She hoped to alleviate any awkwardness by finding common ground through music.

"I actually don't know any of those bands. I don't really listen to much music, but I hear a lot of pop because of my younger siblings. It's not really for me, though," he stated, wishing he was more interesting.

Walter fumbled, "Uh, well. Maybe you could . . . I mean, do you have a favorite band?"

Caroline answered with enthusiasm, "Yeah. I'll play you my favorite song 'Star Stella' by Grizzly Outlook when we get inside." The girl eagerly retrieved a CommX9 from the storage pocket of her chair. Walter stared in astonishment as Caroline retrieved the latest and greatest piece of technology soon to hit Immerxia.

In a surprising moment of candor, Caroline admitted, "I know. I know. It's not even out yet, but my parents work for CommX. They try to test out a lot of the products on me. It's kind of a waste, though.

I don't really VEX."

While Walter's mouth hung open, Caroline continued, "I basically only use it to call my parents in case of an emergency and listen to my favorite bands."

She began the ascent to the library before suddenly stopping to ask, "Hold on. Why are *you* going to the library? I've never seen you here before. I know it's not for the social scene." She chuckled.

Not wanting to answer any questions, only ask them, Walter instead dodged. "Have you ever met Author here before? Well, that's the name I use."

"Who's Author?" Caroline asked, looking confused. The teenagers reached the entrance to the empty building and paused.

Walter stared at Caroline and wondered how to explain Author. "Well, it's hard to describe Author. Kinda tall but not too tall. Lighter than me but darker than you. Medium build. Seems to know way too much about me. Actually, seems to know way too much about everything."

"Oh, I think you mean the librarian that works here. I've never asked for a name. I agree, sure does seem to know a lot, though. Just last week, the librarian suggested I talk to my doctor about a new medication."

Caroline stopped herself from sharing further. She had let her guard down in Walter's friendly presence, but she felt she had shared too much again with the burgeoning friend. She continued with discretion, "Strangely enough, I had never discussed my health with the librarian. It wouldn't be the first time I'd thought maybe the cataloger was a mind reader, though. Sometimes, a question comes to me while I'm reading, and usually, soon after, the librarian gives an answer to the question I never asked aloud. Every once in a while, I'll go check to see if the answer was right. Sure enough, it's always correct. If I didn't know any better, it's like this librarian wrote the books rather than archived them."

"That's crazy. Seemed to know a lot about me too. Also, something impossible happened to me today, and I think . . . maybe . . . possibly, Author was somehow behind it," Walter hedged. He was not particularly familiar with this classmate, but he found himself caring more and more about what she thought of him.

Caroline wheeled to the heavy, revolving door. She pushed a small inlaid stained glass panel to start a slow and consistent rotation. Walter followed her into the dimly lit Xitus Library. In the short time between visits, he had forgotten the magical quality of the bygone property. In particular, the stained glass windows appeared more vibrant than before, as the sun was shining brighter.

Walter paused to study the depicted scenes. The eye-catching glass seemed almost life-like as did the characters portrayed. They were so realistic, Walter almost believed they could step out of their large gothic frames.

"They're beautiful, aren't they? Not to weird you out, but I've always thought this one looks a little bit like you. Not that I think you're beautiful or anything . . . I mean, you're . . . no that's not what I mean . . . I mean—" Caroline stopped as her cheeks became warm.

In his own embarrassment, Walter turned his gaze to the character in the image. She wasn't wrong. The person rendered shared the same build, stature, and features as the teenage boy. For Walter, it was as if he was staring into a twenty-foot mirror. Yet, he could not identify the images of the three strangers standing alongside his likeness.

Walter's eyes carried to the subsequent scenes. These depictions were much more fantastical. Floating land masses. Light and dark creatures. Fiery chaos. Before Walter could continue his survey, Caroline interrupted with a dust-induced sneeze.

"I just wheeled around the first floor, and I didn't see the librarian. I'm not surprised we're the only visitors here, but the librarian is always nearby. I've never had trouble finding your Author. Why don't we check the second floor? I'll take the ancient elevator on the left if you take the stairs on the right."

The kids split in different directions. Walter hurried toward the stairwell, hoping to find Author first. He had a lot of questions and wanted to ask them out of earshot of Caroline. Walter reached the ornate oak door leading to the stairs and briefly noticed another inlaid stained glass panel. The image was of beautiful and illuminated rolling hills. In his rush, he did not take the time to appreciate the full splendor of the small colorful window.

The determined youth climbed the stairs toward the second floor. Unexpectedly, Walter noticed strings of light sway three steps above him. He figured the play of light was from one of the many windows in the library; even the stairwell was lined with enameled glass. Almost as suddenly as he noticed the irradiance, Walter climbed into a foreign but peculiarly familiar place. He thought it was eerily similar to the stained glass he passed in the staircase door. All Walter could see in front of him were miles of hills and valleys covered in luminescent alien flora.

"Nice to see you again, Walter. Welcome to Animus." Walter was startled at the sound of Author's voice behind him.

Lumen were loyal to a fault. There was no defecting or deserting, no matter the cost. A few dozen of the radiant beings watched as the second child of the day entered Animus. They looked to one another, acknowledging the importance of their devotion to Author and the text. Now more than ever, in the beginning of the end, the Lumen recognized their critical supporting role in restoring the world.

Low and slow notes began to flow from a Lumen standing guard at one of the loci. As each beacon heard the call, the next in line would join the response. The message was passed along. Every third Lumen stepped forward to begin to make a vast perimeter around Walter and Author. The boy was here, and the Murk were approaching. It was time to sacrifice it all.

13

ANIMUS MONDAY 6:04 P.M.

● ● ●

"WELP, THIS SEEMS about right. This day just keeps getting weirder. Author, I haven't known you long, but you continue to outdo yourself with twists," Walter said, scratching his head. He did not expect to end up in a seemingly different world face-to-face with Author, although in retrospect, maybe he should have.

The smiling being responded, "Oh, I am only getting started. Life with me is anything but commonplace. Only a fool casts me as a boring dinosaur."

For the first time, Walter took a moment to closely survey his surroundings. The first thing that caught the lost boy's eyes were small technicolor lights crawling around his feet and excitedly buzzing passed his nose. Focusing on this rainbowed light show, Walter discovered these were none other than bioluminescent insects, known as embers. Walter looked for Author's reaction and noticed the bugs fluttered around and landed on the calm presence's dark-green combat jacket. Almost immediately upon touching down, the critters on the being began to simultaneously flash the same sequence of colors. Author appeared unphased by this display and focused on lightning strikes in the distance instead.

Tapping into his other senses, Walter breathed deep the cool air. There was a faint scent of peppermint and lemon. Bending down to touch the silky vegetation and velvety insects, thoughts of

Stacey crept back into his mind. He knew none of her other suitors could top this breathtaking experience. The more Walter thought, though, the more he questioned who he actually wanted to share this moment with. The events of the day and his unfettered ease with Caroline pushed Stacey to the periphery.

Cutting in on Walter's rumination, Author bluntly stated, "You are right to doubt her importance in your life. She is not worth the space you allow her in your mind."

Frustrated by the unsolicited advice, Walter blurted, "Since you obviously know everything, just tell me what I'm doing here. No more riddles. No more games. I just want some answers." Immediately, the adolescent was ashamed of his moodiness toward the writer of everything.

Sensing the tense situation, the embers cooled their colors and quickly flew away. "No need to feel bad. I've heard much worse. I understand the unraveling of your reality is maddening, but truth has a silly way of overwhelming your sensibilities. In the grand scheme of things, the hours of today have taken centuries for me to formulate. Believe me when I say, what you are waiting for is worth it. Please wait a little longer. We do not have our whole party here yet, although they should be close."

Still regretful of his words to the humble deity, Walter thought before he spoke again. Choosing his next words with his emotions in check, he asked, "Who are we waiting for? More people like you? More people like me?"

"My boy, there is no one like me. I think you are beginning to learn that. We are waiting for the other protagonists. I have bound your futures together for the restoration of the world. The task is too great for any one of you alone," Author said with solemn compassion.

Walter asked, "Is the world really so bad that it needs to be restored?" The sincerity with which the seventeen-year-old asked his question made him appear older and wiser.

"That is the answer you must all hear together. How about I tell you some stories while we wait? I do love to tell my stories. I think you will find these illuminating. Please take a seat." Author paused and motioned for the guest to sit.

Before Walter's eyes, the ground cover slowly grew into two lounge chairs facing each other. The teenager sunk into the plush leaves that formed the cushions. He placed his hands on the arm rests made of thick swirling vines. It was the most comfortable seat Walter had ever eased into.

Author began, "There once was a mother that had seven daughters. Each girl was unique and brought the mother much joy. One by one, the daughters became young women and moved away from their mother. The oldest daughter gained great power, but she held it over many people. The second daughter found many hardships, and she lived only to survive. The third daughter accumulated much wealth, but she kept it all for herself. The middle daughter neither thrived nor languished, and she lived a mediocre life. The fifth daughter was an influential speaker, but she used her voice only for her own advancement. The sixth daughter coveted all that others had, and she overlooked the good in her own life. The youngest daughter did not care for earthly ambitions like the others, and the world rejected her."

Author continued, "Over the years, each of the daughters became like strangers to one another, and they forgot about their mother. The world became too much for them, and what was most important was forgotten. Ever still, the mother loved them all and tried to usher them home to her."

The orator then posed a couple of questions. "Should the mother no longer love her children? Should the mother simply move on?"

Without waiting for a reply, Author began a second story. "There once was a man that traveled in darkness and desired a way to light his journey. He went from city to city searching for various forms of light to brighten his path. The smallest city provided the traveler with a matchbook, and the man saw a short distance in front of himself.

The second city handed him a candle, and he carried the light with him. The third city gave the nomad an oil lantern, and he controlled the flame's brilliance. The next city contributed a flare to the man, and others saw him coming from a great distance away. The fifth city donated a flashlight to the wanderer, and his light lasted for weeks. The sixth city presented the wayfarer with a solar light, and the man's radiant source was renewed each day. The last city, the most advanced of all, handed the journeyman a bottled star, and he had light to the end of his days. Reflecting on his life, the man concluded that all the sources of light were spectacular, and he appreciated each one."

The storyteller again asked rhetorical questions. "Is not each form of light special? Do they all not ward off darkness?"

Again, Author did not wait for an answer and continued with more tales. Walter listened intently and nodded along with minimal understanding. He hoped that the meaning of his host's words would soon be revealed.

The chronicles of the planes were many, but there was one that shifted the course of humanity unlike any other. Long ago, the world was full of tranquility, harmony, and goodness. In Pax, the world was new. The days stretched forever, and night never fell. Paxians walked the knolls picking the life-sustaining vegetation. Lumen were born from the good acts of the Paxians and lived amongst them. Their melodious conversations filled the air with sweet music.

But with humans, there is always a desire for opposition, for distinction. The unraveling began with one small comment that was bred from the falsehood of self-importance. "I hate them." In that moment, the first Murk was born. With wide eyes, the present Paxians watched as a dark form materialized in the air where the words still hung. The sky's brilliance lowered as the first storm appeared in Pax above the Murk.

The obscure figure reflected the appearance of Kieran, the nidus of the evil words. The Paxians looked upon the obscured representation with intrigue. This would not be the last time Kieran conceived another wicked embodiment. In fact, Paxians would breed scores of Murk.

14

● ● ●

THE GIRLS WALKED down the tunnel slope to The Core. The walls were adorned with large, rusted lanterns that flickered and lit spectacular murals. The massive, spray-painted scenes told the stories of the Forgotten. To anyone familiar with Euporia, they would imagine sorrowful chronicles of the underground inhabitants, but the tales were largely joyful. Dez barely slowed her tempo, but Arabella lagged behind, mesmerized by this subterranean world.

Arabella was particularly interested in a piece of sprayed art that depicted a crowd dancing underneath the stars. These stars were like nothing she had ever seen before. The lights were colorful, undulating, and centered above the people. The rest of the scene was jet-black, making the vivid celestial body the most prominent feature.

"Hey! Keep up. It's a labyrinth down here. If you get lost, I won't find you for days," Dez shouted back. Arabella ran down the stairs carved into the bedrock of the tunnel, taking two at a time, to rejoin her awaiting guide. At the base of the steps was a large wooden sign that read *The Forgotten Core: Always Open. Always Welcome.*

The tunnel opened into a never-ending corridor lined with varying carts and booths. Every wall in sight was covered in the signature street art. Despite the late hour, the interconnecting hallways were bustling with people dressed in brightly colored and handmade attire. Interspersed were others dressed in the same drab uniform as Dez. These E-Corp employees moved quickly with their heads down, hoping not to be spotted by other colleagues. Despite the better quality of the black-market goods, the techies were ashamed to buy goods from the Forgotten.

To Arabella, there appeared to be no rhyme or reason to the placement of the vendors or their commodities. She fell behind again as she enjoyed the sights around her. The obvious tourist watched as one person bought a Forgotten-designed computer next to another that bought Forgotten-grown carrots. Euporians could find anything in The Market if they knew where to look.

Arabella easily found Dez dressed in her ripped uniform, walking through the sea of uniquely adorned individuals. Dez walked toward a booth with a sign stating *Good Feels.* Standing behind the plastic counter of the booth was a striking woman in her twenties. Her skin tone matched those painted on the muralled walls of the tunnel the teens had just descended. Even her hair appeared painted with the colors of the rainbow. Arabella had passed many people in this strange and exciting place, but no one quite this eccentric. She'd never felt further from the clean-cut Aurelia.

"Hey, stranger. Long time no see," the beautiful woman behind the counter called out to Dez.

"Hey, Sophia. It *has* been a while. I've been working late recently. Gotta get my productivity numbers up," Dez said with an eye roll.

"I've been telling you for years to just come join me down here. You could have a booth right next to mine. Life above is not all it's cracked up to be. You know that. They are wasting your talents, but you could make a real difference down here," Sophia said.

After hearing the hard truth, Dez responded defensively, "My parents would never make it without my health insurance through E-Corp and the medicines above. You know they both have Euporian Exhaustion. Life isn't all good feels. You know that better than anyone else. You've never had more customers."

Not wanting to remain a fly on the wall, Arabella interjected with her usual politeness. "Hi. I'm Arabella. Can you help me? I don't have any emergency money that I can use to get home, but you can have this." Arabella removed the beautiful Aurelian flag gold pin from her dress and laid it on the counter in front of Sophia.

Ignoring the payment, Sophia stated, "Of course, I can help you. I can help everyone as long as they search for me. You have found me, which is more than many people. Remember, though, it is one thing to find me, but it is another to accept my help. Many people seek me for the quick-fix pills, but I try to tell them that my words are the medicine they seek. Engaging in conversation with me and heeding my advice can guide seekers down the right path."

She continued, "For instance, take Dez. She visits for the sake of her parents, but she does not receive help for herself. She is tied to the terrible conditions above ground because they are familiar, and she is unwilling to risk moving to The Core. If she did, Dez would be an unstoppable force."

Shocked by the woman's candor, Arabella asked, "Do you know where Aurelia is? Can you help me get back to my home?"

Smiling, Sophia responded, "I know all about Aurelia and Aurelians, Euporia and Euporians, and Immerxia and Immerxians. But no, I can't get you back home. I *can* get you to somewhere better, or rather, to some*one* better, though."

"There is nowhere better than Aurelia. I just want to go home," Arabella replied almost tearfully.

At that moment, a gruff, bearded E-Corp employee pushed through the inquisitors to Sophia's counter. "I heard from a friend that you sell happiness. It's been a rough couple of days, really a rough couple of years."

Sophia was oddly disappointed with the potential sale opportunity before her. She was more interested in giving wisdom than selling an emotional Band-Aid. The saleswoman began a canned disclaimer given to all first-time customers. "I can sell you artificial relief, but you must know the effect is temporary, and you may feel worse afterwards. I grow all the ingredients in my own garden and purify them in my lab. I do not use any illegal additives, and I can guarantee my products' safety."

Bored with her speech, the customer's eyes glazed over as he peered right through Sophia. She persisted, "This is not true happiness; a pill can only do so much. Happiness only comes from giving up the pursuits of this world. If you would like, I can tell you more. My friend Dez here can assist as well. She's much more capable than she looks." Sophia gestured toward the disheveled girl with the torn sleeve.

Backing away from the conversation, Dez blurted, "Leave me out of this! I keep telling you, I had nothing to do with that woman getting better a couple months ago."

The customer was all too happy to ignore Sophia's suggestion. "Just sell me the pill so I can get out of this pit."

Sophia searched through the dispensable pills for the requested medication. Under the clear counter, each pill was a different color and with a different small picture displayed on its coating. She reluctantly retrieved a small yellow pill with a smiley face printed on the surface. "E-Corp credits are no good down here, but what information can you offer me as payment? Knowledge is better than money."

The downtrodden man sighed as he put his E-Corp wallet back in his E-Corp satchel. "I figured that would be the case." Before contributing confidential information about his employer, the man looked around the bustling market for other colleagues. Seeing none nearby, he divulged, "I'm a tech in the civil engineering department. Partial plans came across my computer recently for a new factory above *this place*. It would require filling in the main tunnel entrance to support the massive foundation."

"Thank you for this information," Sophia stoically responded. She handed the man his purchased tablet. Without another word, and with the pill clutched tight in his fist, the man retreated into the crowd. "Usually, the information offered is not that helpful. I'll have to spread the word. Now, back to what's important," she said, addressing the girls.

"Okay, Sophia. Stop playing games. We need your help," Dez exclaimed.

"I know you do. It's just that I've missed our fellowship. I know much of what you need to know, but I must send you to the one who knows far more than I do."

Becoming impatient, Arabella questioned, "How do we find this person? I just want to go home."

"Really, you already know them, even if you don't know that you know them. You just do not know how to find them. Here's how you do that. You must cross a locus to Animus. There are many loci, but each one takes you to a different location in Animus. Go to the edge of The Market. I have a hunch this locus will take you where you need to go."

Looking straight at Arabella, Sophia added, "Something tells me you've already been to Animus. You will find a locus in the garden of wild blaze that separates The Market from nearby housing. The vegetation will be flashing, so you can't miss the spot."

"Locus? Blaze? Animus? This is weird even for you," Dez joked in disbelief.

Even though Arabella was unfamiliar with the expansive underground community, she sprinted in the direction Sophia was pointing, leaving her valuable pin behind. She navigated through the maze of The Core as if her feet already knew the way. Dez ran after Arabella. Seemingly by luck, the outsider found the garden of blaze. The local did not catch up until the Aurelian was at the back of the garden, reaching toward linear strands of light suspended above the iridescent plants.

Dez grabbed hold of Arabella's remaining hand in Euporia. Before Dez could stop her, she was pulled into another world.

Lux appeared at the entrance of The Market at the exact moment when Dez and Arabella began their downward climb. The stellar form hung close to the muralled walls, changing colors like a chameleon mimicking the art. Just in the periphery of the girls, Lux gave a quick flash of light above a particular painting.

Lux knew the prompt was successful when Arabella stopped next to the seminal work. The heavenly figure hovered just above the surface of the starry depiction of itself. Arabella only noticed the two-dimensional picture of Lux as the real Lux hid in plain sight. The cosmic body observed Arabella as she graciously admired the new concepts introduced to her unknowingly small world.

As the heroines traversed through The Core, Lux followed inconspicuously. While approaching Sophia's booth, Lux sensed imminent danger. The ever-perceptive constellation discerned the Switcher at work in Euporia. Dozens of E-Corp security, more ominously known as the E-Corp Brigade, were headed to apprehend Dez. By now, E-Corp had detected her unauthorized use of their computer hardware.

Lux fluctuated above the conversation at the booth and kept watch for the quickly approaching henchmen. Thankfully, the dialogue ended, and Lux was already in position to lead Arabella to the locus. No longer desiring to hide, Lux shone brightly above her. The guide led the unwitting girl through the maze of booths into the garden before zipping through the curtain separating the worlds.

15

"WELL DONE!" AUTHOR stated enthusiastically to Arabella and Dez just moments after arriving in Animus. The disoriented girls stared blankly at the all-knowing being. "Good. All my protagonists are together. I guess I should make formal introductions. Dez, this is Walter, and you already know Arabella. Arabella, you already know Dez, but this is Walter. And Walter, meet Dez and Arabella." The clueless teens smiled awkwardly at each other.

Continuing on as the only willing speaker, Author addressed Lux. "Friend, I can always count on you to be the best guide. Even in danger, you don't fail me." Lux gave two bright flashes in acknowledgment and appreciation. "The Switcher has fully infiltrated E-Corp and is using its security for the foulest of work. Thank you for retrieving them before matters escalated."

Walter was the first of the kids to speak, being the most acquainted with Author. Nervously, the boy began, "Author, where are we, and what are we doing here? Just hours ago, I was in the library. Since I got here, you've dodged all my questions and continued to tell me stories while we waited. Is this who we were waiting for?"

"Yeah, we were just in The Core talking to Sophia. Where are we?" Dez asked. "And by the way, who are *you*?"

Author calmly and kindly replied, "Sophia is a good friend of mine, much closer than most. She dispenses much more than fleeting relief. I'm glad you listened to her." It was not lost on the adolescents that Author did not answer their questions.

Silence fell amongst the group. In the moments that passed, the teens measured up each part of their triad. Each concluded that none of their counterparts appeared that special. They all looked pretty ordinary and were skeptical of their bond. Author had intentionally brought the three together, but why?

Their apparent leader stood in the middle of a vast plain covered in wild blaze. Author gestured for the youth to sit. As before, the plush and flashing vegetation formed chairs for each party. The teens nervously eyed a storm raging in the distance as they sat down. "I've looked forward to this day for centuries. We have a lot to discuss and very little time, so let me begin."

Taking a seat with the group, Author pressed on. "Over the years, I have been called many things. I allow those that directly communicate with me to choose what name best suits me. I met Walter just earlier today, and Walter chose to call me Author. This name is quite fitting, since I wrote everything into existence, and nothing is untouched by my ink. So, if you don't mind, let's stick with the name Author." The teens nodded in agreement, seemingly transfixed.

"The planes that each of you know are relatively new. Well, at least newer in the grand scheme of things. They all originated from a world called Pax. For years, Paxians were righteous people. Their good deeds created the Lumen that lived in their company. Lumen were living representations of the Paxians' virtuous acts. Every good action created a new Lumen, and their numbers multiplied."

Author studied the eyes of the trio for a few seconds to make sure their attention was fully captured.

"Paxians could not find contentment. Happiness became boring, and joy became dull. Evil took root in their hearts, and the first person to commit evil found it stirring. After those first unholy words were spoken, a new creature was unleashed—the Murk. Evil was contagious, and the poisonous representations of Paxians grew rapidly among them."

The adolescents all reacted differently. Arabella, being the youngest, was visibly shaken. Dez, prone to distrust, had a look of disbelief. And Walter, the most even-keeled, was just happy to finally get some answers.

Author continued, "The first Murk grew in prestige and power. This influential original Murk became known as the Switcher. It is the most wicked villain of all time. This creature tempted Paxians to do evil, so more Murk were created for an army. Its goal was to rid the world of Paxians and their Lumen and possess Pax for itself. Evil became so rampant that the Murk began to overpower the Lumen and extinguish them. The Paxians began to destroy each other and their world. They were well on their way to self-destruction."

Author paused, head bowed and looking solemn. "The world I had lovingly written into existence was crumbling under the weight of the darkness of people. Pax cared for its inhabitants even though they did not care for it, so I allowed Pax to divide its atmosphere, which created the three separate planes that exist today. The world split itself to try to slow the destruction and harm done by humans. Animus, what you see before you, is all that is left of the original Pax.

"Here, the Lumen guard the loci, and the Murk are prevented from interacting with people in their planes. While the supernaturals are stuck here, the actions of people in the planes still create Lumen and Murk in Animus and affect the stability of the atmosphere. The Switcher was meant to be trapped here as well, but it created an escape route from its prison. There are consequences on this means of evasion, though. Crossing out of the atmosphere of Animus forces the Switcher to take the form of a human being in each plane, which reduces its supernatural power."

Author's narrative struck a chord with Dez and her reality in Euporia. Hungry for more information, she asked bluntly, "Do I know the Switcher? Do any of us know the Switcher?"

With a reassuring tone, Author responded, "Dez, do not worry.

You will get the answers to your questions, but I am a writer, and I must not skip any pages in the story." Author continued, "The spread of evil slowed by breaking Paxians into three smaller groups, and the three planes were filled with ex-Paxians. The three planes are the ones you know today: Euporia, Aurelia, and Immerxia. This happened so long ago, it is ancient history. It is told as folklore in some small circles, but is largely dismissed as mythology."

Author went on to explain the geographical phenomenon surrounding them. "The planes exist entangled together with Animus. It keeps the planes invisible and isolated from the others. But from inside Animus, at any time, you can see the overlapping planes at a single point."

All the teenagers turned their heads in different directions to observe the spectacle. With this new understanding, and at Author's revealing, the young people saw the looming skyscrapers of Euporia, the picturesque parks of Aurelia, and the cookie-cutter neighborhoods of Immerxia overlapping before their eyes. "So, that's what I saw when I was here last time," Arabella declared emphatically.

"As you can see, the world is much more complex than any of you could imagine. Now, you must be wondering why you're here, and why I'm telling you all of this. You were all written into existence for a purpose, a world-changing purpose. I knew that people would not be able to defeat evil on their own, and you would be necessary to save them. Each of you has a special ability, even if you do not know or acknowledge it yet. I know this may be hard to believe, but trust me, I am the one who developed your characters."

Looking directly at Dez, Author said, "Destiny, you have the power to heal the ones around you. Remember Val and the woman in The Market? You truly alleviated their distress. This is just the beginning of your gift. If you learn the worth and value I gave you, then you will be able to heal people across every plane."

Before Dez could respond, Author turned toward the young man. "Walter, you have the power to alter and manifest tangible objects.

Today, you really did materialize a meal for your hungry classmate. This is small in comparison to what you can do. If you trust my truth, you will be able to turn valleys into hills and flatten mountains."

Finally, Author turned toward the youngest of the group. "Arabella, you have the power to foresee moments in the future. Does this encounter not seem familiar to you? You've dreamt this moment many times before. Your dreams are glimpses into the future. Before my ink even dries, you know what I have written to come. If you can let go of your world and rely on us, then you will be able to manipulate the future." Arabella's eyes widened as she was finally able to discern the words spoken so many times in her most frequent, recurring dreams.

Walter asked the question aloud all three teenagers were thinking, "Why us? Why not someone older or with more influence?"

Author answered, "Each person I write into existence is a word in my chronicles, and they have the ability to guide their own story. But each of you is not just a word but a coauthor. My ink courses through your veins, gives you life, and allows you to produce works. You don't need to be older, and you already have the influence you need. You have the ability to cowrite the ending of this story with me. The three of you together can alter the past, present, and future. I wove your gifts into these final chapters of my masterpiece."

The determined speaker continued to persuade the attentive teens. "The inhabitants of the planes need you and your gifts, now more than ever. They were meant for so much more than what they have become, but you can restore them. It starts with you being their virtuous example. Can you imagine? To build a community founded on love rather than vices? To embrace differences rather than wage wars over them? To care for the other rather than cast them aside? This is possible, and so much more, with you leading the way. Teach them there is another way, a better way, to live."

Suddenly, Author's piercing gaze focused on flashes of lightning in the distance. "I know this is a lot for you three to take in, but you must use your gifts to transform your planes. Only with these talents will victory be possible. To win the battle, you must help people fight for righteousness so their acts of good prevail over evil. From this, you will ensure Lumen outnumber the Murk and develop the army you need. Only then will the Switcher be defeated and the planes restored.

"Battles are happening here, but soon, they will begin in your planes. Without my Lumen guarding the loci, and without the atmosphere separating the planes from Animus, people will inevitably face the Murk. Know, this will be dangerous. The Switcher is powerful and has infiltrated each plane deeply. Many people will be deceived into looking for you and helping our adversary. People will turn on each other, but they will especially turn on you. But be encouraged, you are destined to succeed. There will be setbacks along the way, but these will not prevent your inevitable victory."

Author studied the teens' faces and then offered, "I cannot make you partake in this fight. It must be your own choice. Be assured, light may seem fickle when it flickers and flutters, but oh, it is much more powerful than dark when it is freed. It adapts, it changes, and it grows. Darkness stays stagnant and depends on the absence of light. Light always has the potential to overcome darkness, if only we allow it.

"Also, know that I will not abandon you on this mission, and I will be with you every step of the way. I know you have many more questions, but you will understand much more over time. Now, you must decide. Will you join me? Will you prolifically fill the blank pages?"

The storm drew nearer. Each of the chosen triad stood and faced their captain. Each thought hard about the story woven before them. Each made up their mind.

After a few moments passed, Walter took a deep breath and spoke first. "I'm in. Immerxians may be lost, but I don't think they're a lost cause. I couldn't live with myself if I did nothing despite knowing I could help."

Timidly, Arabella followed. "Author, I'm ready to start. I'm nervous to leave Aurelia, but I know that if I don't fight, there might not be an Aurelia to go back to. I want to save my home and my people."

After a dramatic silence, all eyes were on Dez. She had the least to lose and so little to go back to. Her eyes fell to the poem scrawled under her ripped sleeve. "There is little to feel in Euporia but despair, but for the first time in my life, you have made me feel hope. I can't walk away from this feeling. Let's do this."

Lux responded to their affirmative answers with a bright sustained burst of light. Their excitement grew as their bond was cemented. Author showed little surprise at the courage displayed. "Good. You will be my Intrepid Three. We must begin immediately. It's time to sharpen your skills and make allies."

Before Author could continue, streams of light emanated from the atmosphere as it began to part in the middle of the circled assemblage.

After a slow ascent in the vintage Xitus Library elevator, Caroline used her hands to slide the metal gates outward. She propelled herself off the elevator and looked across the second floor. It only took a few moments to scan the entirety of the balconied story. Similar to the first, the most prominent feature of the second floor was the continuation of the stained glass scenes. Walter was nowhere to be seen or heard.

"Walter, where are you? This isn't funny," Caroline called out. Not hearing a response, Caroline peered through the bars of the wrought iron balcony railing suspended above the stacks. Walter being nowhere in sight, she muttered under her breath, "Of course, just like a boy to leave you hanging." After scanning the second floor once more, she quizzically stated, "He's got to be around here somewhere." Suddenly, from the opposite side of the library, Caroline heard a loud slam echo downstairs. She thought she saw another one of her classmates enter the stairwell.

The individualist, not wanting to just stand around and wait, set off around the second story in search of the stairwell. Abandoning the rickety elevator, for now, Caroline decided to head toward the stairwell, where she hoped to meet Walter on the upper landing. There was a small stained glass window inlaid in the oak door to the stairwell. The art depicted the backs of three young adults sitting in front of a figure that was uncannily similar to the librarian.

Caroline gave a tug on the heavy wooden door and quickly drove herself onto the stairway, landing and narrowly avoiding the swinging door. Steadying at the edge of the stairs, she noticed light refracting through dust particles in the air. The beams formed uniform columns. With an outstretched hand, Caroline reached for one of the cords. Her wheels lurched forward and shockingly threw her body and wheelchair into an outdoor nightscape instead of crashing down the library stairs.

The ever-adventurous Caroline gracefully landed upright and in her chair. The deep groundcover slowed her momentum and protectively wrapped her spokes with its vines. As the Xitus Library disappeared behind her, she marveled at the scene before her – hills of vegetation that flashed a kaleidoscope of color and brewing storms in every direction. The pulsating and fluctuating lights were mesmerizing as she trudged up a hill.

Reaching the top, the faint outline of four beings interrupted her gaze.

16

ANIMUS MONDAY 11:11 P.M.

THE GROUP STOOD aghast as the atmosphere parted and unveiled Immerxia. Walter recognized the slick marble stairs of the Xitus Library interior. He even heard Caroline faintly shout, "Where are you?" A young female silhouette approached the open locus.

To Walter's shock, Caroline did not appear in Animus. Instead, the form of another young woman slowly dissipated as it passed through the atmosphere to expose a tall and looming figure. In the girl's place was the shadowy representation of the first transgressor, which floated slightly above the blaze. The vegetation appeared to lose its glow below the being. A scent of decay started to fill the onlookers' nostrils.

The teens were horrified to look upon the Switcher. Its face was hollow and sunken. There were no eyes within the sockets. The being appeared soulless, barely resembling its human originator. Instead, it encompassed the grotesqueness of every bad actor in history. A dark fog filled the air within the Switcher's frame. Swinging from its gaunt body were all forms of restraints—chains and ropes of various sizes—symbolizing the tethering of odious human souls to their master.

"Hello, my old *friend*. Are these your selected heroes? They look *formidable*. My worry was not wasted," the Switcher stated facetiously in a gravelly voice to Author. Unlike the less powerful Murk, the Switcher was able to speak words. "I see that they call you Author. How fitting. I could think of a few less flattering terms."

Author ignored the nemesis's greeting and kept watching the protagonists. The Switcher continued, "By now, *Author* has surely told you how *terrible* I am, and how I must be stopped. Well, let me formally introduce myself. I am known as the Switcher. Or, as I like to call myself, the Lord of Chaos." It emitted an evil laugh. The teenagers looked to Author for guidance, but their leader did not react to the Switcher's words.

The Switcher rolled on. "I was born out of the first wicked words uttered by a human. It was a world-altering decision of that Paxian to breathe evil into existence. They did not know they would create me, but wasn't that a lucky consequence? Fortunately for me, it is enticing to be bad, so evil spread within them and throughout the land of Pax. With every contemptible action, a Murk was created, so I did very little work to create my own army. As you can see, people have been very bad." The Switcher motioned behind it to the rows of Murk falling into formation.

As Dez, Arabella, and Walter realized this terrifying creature was hauntingly familiar, the haughty Switcher stated, "Well, that's enough of a history lesson. I think we all get it. People are bad, Murk are created, and I grow in power. There is no reason for me to lie to you. I want the world for myself. So, how about the big reveal? Would you like to know who I am to each of you? We all have an intimate connection. By my own design, of course."

Offering a chance of reprieve, Author interjected, "My Intrepids, these next words spoken to you will be hard to hear, but it is vital you know. Remember, nothing falls outside of my plot. As always, I am here with you, and you have nothing to fear." Directing attention to the Switcher, Author warned, "Tread carefully. We both know I can end this moment in an instant."

With what resembled a mouth, an empty cavern on its face, the Switcher attempted a sneering smile. "Friend, you know I only want what is best for them. I will be gentle with my delivery," the Switcher lied.

"Oldest first. Would you like to guess, Walter? Or should I say *Wally*?" As the Switcher spoke Walter's nickname, the creature morphed into the dark silhouette of a short teenage girl. Its voice perfectly mimicked Walter's crush. The figment floated inches from Walter's face, taunting him.

"That's impossible. I've known Stacey since grade school," Walter gasped at the appalling betrayal.

"Time is my friend, and patience is my ally. My plan started many centuries ago. I've lived countless personas that spanned a human's lifetime. Do you think a single childhood is of any consequence to me, Wally? What do you truly know of Stacey? Have you met her family? Have you seen her house? Your innocence made you gullible and easily fooled," the Switcher bragged.

Walter hung his head, feeling ashamed and embarrassed. To ensure it delivered blows as quickly as possible, the Switcher turned its attention to Dez. As it began to speak, the dark silhouette shifted to a lumbering man with a booming voice. Dez immediately recognized Mr. Rothchild. "Oh, EC3315763, ruling over you was particularly satisfying. Isn't your life just terrible? And to think, a chance at happiness was right under your feet. You naively believed E-Corp would eventually benefit your parents' lives, but E-Corp was created by me to benefit me and only me."

Not wanting to be encumbered by her E-Corp identity, Dez completely ripped off her already dangling sleeve. In her anger, she balled up the jacket piece and threw it at the insidious brute. The sleeve harmlessly passed through the Switcher and hit the ground with Dez's identification patch faceup. Red-faced, she yelled, "You tyrant! You've created all our suffering!"

"Oh no, my valued member, Euporians, as all humans, created their own suffering. I just nudged people in the right, I mean, *wrong* direction." Keeping the momentum, the Switcher finally focused on Arabella. "Ah, the youngest. This confession is going to be particularly cathartic. I'm immensely proud of how close I was able to get to you."

The girl's hands trembled as she looked to Author for comfort. With a pat of the chest and a reassuring nod, Author provided the support needed. Arabella tightened her fists at her side to steady her hands. She was ready to hear the ominous news.

The Switcher shifted its form once again as it began to hum an intimate tune, "A Daughter's Dance." The dark silhouette changed into a previously reassuring profile. "Hello, my precious daughter. Would you like to take a walk to Gryffin Park with me?" spoken in Caius's voice.

Arabella's face twisted in anguish, tears rolling down her cheeks. The father she once loved was a farce. The young teen had never experienced heartbreak until now. The weight of this news sat heavy on her. Reveling in this reaction, the Switcher gleefully offered more devastation. "Don't cry, my child. It's not all bad. I'm not actually your biological father. Your upstanding mother had a relationship with a common man before she married me. You are a product of that unspeakable connection in a plane obsessed with status. Thankfully, I was there to swoop in and rescue the family's honor. How silly? To let tradition and formalities determine one's future."

Not believing the Switcher, Arabella quizzed, "If you're telling the truth, then who is my real father? And, what about Maximillian? None of what you say makes sense."

"You're not as smart as I thought if you haven't figured it out yet. Ask your foolish mother. You'll probably be happy to hear that I'm not Maximillian's father either," the creature taunted.

With pain in her voice, Arabella responded, "But my father was so kind and loving to me. Clearly, you're neither."

Caius's avatar grinned and snickered. "Arabella, you're being small-minded. Think about it. I walked you to the park, said a few flowery remarks, and taught you some nice songs. That's it. It was all a means to an end.

"After my 'death' is when I did the real work. I'm most proud of the manufactured journal entries I left for you. Distance makes the heart grow fonder. You have idealized our relationship." The Switcher took great pleasure in twisting the knife deeper into Arabella's heart.

The creature returned to its revolting form. Addressing the group, the Switcher said, "It was all a ruse. I positioned myself in roles of authority or influence in each of your lives to cause as much strife as possible. Arabella, I divided your mind by multiplying your sorrow. Dez, I held your head below water by keeping you above ground. Walter, I pierced through your heart by going around your sensibilities."

"You weren't the only ones I was concerned with, though. I wanted to create as much destruction as possible on each plane, and I've become quite good at that over the last few millennia. In Aurelia, I lulled them into their own complacency through abundance. In Euporia, I struck fear into their lives through oppression. In Immerxia, I overwhelmed them with an abundance of inconsequential information. Really, manipulating the planes was utterly easy. I only employed one tactic in each plane. I am ruthless but calculated in fashioning suffering." The Switcher savored these moments in the spotlight.

Not wanting to entertain the Switcher's madness any longer, Author ended the creature's soapbox monologue. "Enough! You've served your purpose for today. The next time we meet, you will not be so cavalier. Do not underestimate The Intrepid Three."

The trio of teens felt the tension rising between the two powerful beings. Their fear firmly cemented them to the pulsating vegetation. All life in Animus was aware of this pivotal moment. The Murk slowly encroached on the heightened situation. Late to the gathering, Lumen raced over the rolling hills to defend their leader and The Intrepid Three.

As if sensing the danger Arabella was in, Maximillian slipped out of the family compound in search of his big sister. The boy rushed toward Gryffin Park. His sense of worry began to override his short but distinguished gait. Usually after sneaking out, he casually strolled around Aurelia, but it was unlike Arabella to disappear, especially for this long. No call, no message, and no sign of Arabella for at least eight hours.

Along the well-lit road that led to the park, Maximillian perceived flashes of stringed lights in his periphery. There was no time to waste, though, so the brother did not slow his pace. He entered Gryffin Park and searched for his beloved sister across the fifteen acres of trees and ponds. Maximillian continued to notice the peculiar threads of light throughout his search.

Almost ready to give up hope, the child paused as the illuminated ropes swayed directly in front of his face. No longer able to ignore the anomalies, Maximillian focused his attention. The atmosphere flapped open at different points as it waved. The boy stood in front of one of the openings. On the other side of the portal was a creature staring back, and it was unnervingly kindred.

Arabella's little brother was faced with one of his own iniquities in the form of a Murk. Maximillian and his evil refraction maintained an arm's length distance. The dark monstrosity shared the boy's proportions and features. The main difference between the child and his dim reflection was the creature's spectral body. Even from the other side of the locus, Maximillian could tell the Murk possessed an immaterial frame. As the form watched its creator intently, it paced side to side. Waiting.

17

ANIMUS MONDAY 11:47 P.M.

"OUR TIME HAS not concluded. You're not the author of *my* path. I'm quite enjoying myself. Why don't I give your three *children* a sampling of my force?" Without waiting for an answer or giving anyone time to react, the Murk initiated an assault. With giddy anticipation, the Switcher backed away from Author and the impending conflict. It planned to watch and revel from a shielded distance. The Lumen sprinted forward to counter their attack.

As the supernaturals advanced toward one another, Author shouted to The Intrepid Three, "Follow Lux! Hurry!" With feet planted, Author removed the trusted stylus, Calamus, from a concealed jacket pocket. The powerful being held the object up to the oncoming army of Murk, which were only twenty feet away and approaching quickly. With a simple stroke of the instrument, Author erased a single Murk with a slash. Author continued this motion to defeat each nearing enemy.

The gobsmacked teens froze in the middle of the battlefield. It was as if their legs turned into cement. Lux, whose typical dimensions were the size of a duffle bag, had grown to the size of a car. It hovered over the teens while repeatedly flashing a blinding white light to get the three teens' attention.

Dez, the coolest under pressure, grabbed Arabella and Walter and pulled them forward. Lux flew toward the Lumen, leading the unprepared adolescents away from the fight. Before they could reach the safety of their allies, a phalanx of Murk broke rank and ambushed the fleeing party.

Recognizing the sneak attack, Lux cast its light as far as possible, enveloping The Intrepid Three as they escaped. The legion of Murk was surprised by this defensive measure and could not slow their blitz. Dez, Arabella, and Walter braced themselves for the imminent impact. The group of evil soldiers crashed into the light of Lux and immediately collapsed. The three teens did not slow their pace as they looked back upon the lifeless Murk.

The escapees crossed through the first rows and columns of the Lumen's noticeably loose formation. It did not take long for the three promising heroes to run beyond the small company. As Walter quickly assessed their odds of survival, he recognized a stock-still figure on the crest of a nearby hill. The seated girl appeared horrified as she watched the mystifying scene unfold.

The Intrepid Three painstakingly sprinted along the ever-changing gradient of the hills toward the young woman. "Caroline! Go! Caroline!" Walter screamed in horror.

The boy grabbed the handles of his new friend's wheelchair, swiveled it around, and pushed her forward to keep her under the protective cover of Lux. All four of them continued to dart up and down the hills of Animus. On one of their climbs, Walter gasped to the newcomer, "How did you find me?"

"I have no idea. None of this makes sense," Caroline replied breathlessly as she helped propel her wheels forward.

Behind the teens, the supernaturals prepared for impact of their opposing hues. The beings knew the collision of light and dark would create devastating harm. A loud whirring from within the dominating Murk met the beat of deep bass drums from within the Lumen. The Lumen halted and formed a defensive position. As each Lumen joined the growing blockade, they intensified in radiance. The Murk, undeterred, prepared to fire their first round of armament.

Author, having the foresight of the events to come, turned away from the Murk and spotted the retreating group of teenagers. They were safely away from the battle and climbing one of the many hills in Animus. Once again, Author readied Calamus.

Author drew three invisible circles in front of the distant group. Their respective planes clearly appeared before the fleeing crew. The atmosphere opened to Immerxia for Walter and Caroline. Aurelia appeared before Arabella, and Dez could see the Core in Euporia.

Immediately following these motions, Author brought hands together at chest level, still holding Calamus, and quickly flung them apart. Lux multiplied from one celestial body into three. The starry forms continued to protectively hover over all the teens and their loci.

In the same moment, the first wave of the Murk's weaponry came crashing down on the wall of Lumen. The sinister creatures rushed into the wounded ready to devour their enemy. Upon this impact of the gleaming and tenebrous supernaturals, there was a great explosion. A blast wave flattened the vegetation under and around the Lumen and carried beyond the battlefield.

The blast reverberated across Animus and threw the teens back to their separate homes. Lux, in its three embodiments, followed through to the three different planes and quickly closed the loci behind each of them.

Effortlessly moving amongst the casualties, the Murk reached out and drew in the surrounding darkness between their hands. As if the darkness was tangible, the evil beings manipulated it like clay into missiles. Synchronously and without an utterance, the Murk fired off their next volley of darkness. The black projectiles rose like a tsunami, high in the sky.

Within the split second before the impact, the remaining upright Lumen emitted forceful sparks of light from within their bodies. The flickers, which appeared miniscule compared to the Murk's weapons, blazed forward with incredible speed toward the enemy. Upon contact, the tiny flares exploded into great balls of light, engulfing the ill-fated Murk.

The missiles crashed down.

18

DEZ FELT THE familiar ground of The Core's tunnels under her feet and used the force to maintain her stride. Unlike the other teenagers, fear was a constant in Dez's life, so she knew exactly what to do. Run. Dez was propelled forward faster with the fresh memory of the haunting scene. As her feet barely touched the ground, she shouted, "Lux, what just happened?"

Walter and Caroline, with Lux floating above, skidded across the floor of the library. The astute girl recognized the impending collision with the circulation desk, so she locked her wheels to save them from a nasty impact. From the momentum, Caroline tumbled face-first out of her wheelchair and barrel-rolled up to the heavy furniture while Walter flipped head over heels and landed comfortably in the friend's padded chair. Realizing what had just happened, the boy popped up and rushed over to the still girl. Walter gently rolled Caroline to her back.

"If I had known you could make the library this thrilling, I would have gotten you here a long time ago," Caroline quipped.

Astonished at her jocularity, Walter asked, "Are you alright?"

Before she could answer, he gently carried Caroline to her wheelchair. The pair tightly held hands and stared at each other in disbelief. The new sidekick gave a reassuring squeeze to the boy's hands.

Looking up to Lux, Walter inquired, "Lux, what are you doing here?"

Arabella's momentum forced her back into Gryffin Park and coincidentally into her brother's stocky frame. The two children hit the ground with a thud. Realizing who broke her fall, Arabella embraced Maximillian with great emotion. While still in the lush grass, Arabella slightly loosened her grip and said, "Max, I have so much to tell you."

With wide eyes, Maximillian pointed at Lux and exclaimed, "Can you start by telling me what that is?"

"Don't worry, I'll tell you everything," Arabella promised her little brother. Raising her head, she asked, "We have to do something. Lux, what do we do?"

Lux, in its three separate embodiments, bounced above the heads of The Intrepid Three in each plane. The guides heard all their questions and simultaneously communicated with all of the teens, plus Caroline and Maximillian. No noise left the stellar formations, but all five heard their inner voices speak to them with the words of Lux.

The spirit began, "Do not be afraid. You are safe for now. You may be separated by planes, but you are together in task and purpose."

Addressing each member's question, Lux continued, "Dez, you saw the beginning of the great last battle. The warring is still ongoing, and it will continue until you all succeed. Author is untouched and is rallying the remaining Lumen as we speak."

Without hesitation or leaving room for response, Lux pressed on, "Walter, I am here to guide and protect you all. Author, with wisdom, multiplied my single embodiment and separated me into three parts. I am with each of you now and forever, and will always be available."

Lux persisted with a greater emphasis. "Arabella, your task is not small. Author has entrusted you three to restore the world. To begin the restoration, you must find others who will believe in your mission and become transformed in their deeds. And then, you must use your gifts to end the war once and for all. I will help you hone your abilities. Dez, you will heal the physical and emotional scars of people to prepare them to fight. Walter, you will touch and manipulate the tangible world to gain an advantage over your enemy. Arabella, you will use your understanding of the future to warn others of what is to come."

"Who do we approach?" Walter asked.

"Anyone. Everyone. Every person is a word, and every word is precious to Author," Lux said. "Tell all you can of what you now know. It does not matter who they are, what they have done, or how they appear. Oftentimes the people who appear most *righteous* are the ones who need the saving. People have become obsessed with labels, rituals, and dogma, but they do not prove a person's worth or value. You must try with every person, and they must decide for themselves. They may not care for you, but you must care for them.

"The more people who choose to be transformed, the more Lumen will be created, and the more Lumen created, the stronger the force opposing evil. War has already begun in Animus and will soon come to all the planes. We need as many people and their Lumen as possible to fight for humanity."

The soundless voice continued, "Now, you will need help with this challenging mission. I implore that you select a few trusted individuals to be your companions and support along this difficult path. This will not be as easy as it sounds. They have not seen what you have seen, nor heard what you have heard. But these exceptional friends will sharpen your abilities to pierce through wickedness. I will also guide and protect those who decide to accompany you."

Lux, in three bodies, moved with unity and fluidity in the three separate planes throughout the entire conversation. The cosmic constellation twinkled, almost as if winking, as it said, "Walter and Arabella, I believe you may have your first volunteers already. If they are willing, Caroline and Maximillian will be invaluable to you."

Their hearts and minds all fell silent.

Caroline was stunned. Usually, her days were uneventful, but today held enough events for a lifetime. Earlier, she believed the highlight of her day was the burgeoning friendship with a cute classmate, but that notion was quickly dispelled after traveling between planes, seeing a supernatural battle, and hearing the voice of Lux within herself.

In the moments after Lux's conclusion, Caroline wondered how she fit with The Intrepid Three. Ever since the illness that took her ability to walk, Caroline had been treated by everyone with kid gloves. Her parents were overly protective, but even still, she attempted more than most Immerxians glued to their technology. The library afforded her the space and autonomy to learn and try new skills. Even if no one knew, Caroline excelled in most things that she tried—languages, instruments, and adaptive exercises, to name just a few.

The brilliant girl always believed she was capable of more than how others treated her, but was she up to this task, was anyone? Caroline looked down at her hand in Walter's. He seemed to believe in her, Lux did too, but most importantly, in that moment, the dauntless teen realized there was no one more able.

19

● ● ●

IN AURELIA, ARABELLA spoke first. "Max, I could really use your help."

Maximillian ribbed, "Oh, *now* you need your little brother's help. You and the sparkly lightshow?" Arabella giggled for the first time since breakfast yesterday. "Can it get me out of homework? Well, who cares, this sounds like fun to me," Maximillian said with a smirk.

"We better get back home," Arabella insisted. "I bet you snuck out too, and it's almost morning. Mom probably has the whole agency looking for us. I'll start to tell you what you need to know on the way back. We'll make our plans while we're grounded."

In Immerxia, Caroline finally broke from her thoughts and released Walter's hand. He knelt in front of her and put a hand on her knee. "What else do you need to know? I'm going to need your help. I have a feeling you have a big part to play in whatever's about to happen."

There were books strewn all around them from Caroline's crash-landing. To steady himself, Walter rested his free hand on an open book next to the pair. Caroline looked down to see his hand on an atlas. The page was full of renderings of Immerxian lakes. Suddenly realizing their immense thirst, he felt the map drawing up into his hand. The two stared in awe at the object in Walter's palm. The page morphed into a glass of water. Walter passed the cup to Caroline. She took a few large gulps before answering, "How about you tell me how on Immerxia did you do that?"

In Euporia, Dez's feet carried her along the art-filled tunnels. There were no current signs of E-Corp's lackeys, but their presence was still seen. The now abandoned booths of The Market were flipped and ransacked. It was abundantly clear to Dez that the Switcher viewed her and her alliance as an existential threat. Despite the chaos around her, she was strangely at ease after Lux's stirring speech. She finally had something and someone she could believe in. With a clear head, she knew exactly who to run to.

"Leave me the room," Benjamina spoke with such intensity that her imposing detail immediately departed her presence. The slight woman crumpled into her office chair and cried. Arabella was missing. Had she finally pushed too hard? And what did Caius have to do with all of this? Benjamina could not lose another person, not Arabella.

Now, more than ever, the mother was glad she forced her children to wear an Aurelian flag pin, in which Frank Rusco had secretly placed a tracking device. This was the first instance Benjamina needed to activate the technology. The national financier wiped her tears and composed herself.

Using her computer, she waited for the tracker's signal to ping. After a long thirty seconds, a blip appeared on the screen.

A loud knock interrupted Benjamina's worry. An apprehensive security officer peeked around the door. "Ma'am, I'm sorry to intrude, but I have some more bad news. Maximillian is missing too."

20

AURELIA WAS NOW anxious, apprehensive, and paralyzed. In less than twenty-four hours, the illusion of comfort had disappeared. Arabella and Maximillian rushed along the manicured sidewalk of Golden Ray Avenue. They were the only living beings in sight. All Aurelians were shut away in their extravagant mansions. Even the wild animals were hiding.

As the siblings neared their home, Lux faded its brilliance to match the stone edifice of the property. Like every other house on the street, the ornate gate to the children's property was secured. Frank Rusco's face peered round the guardhouse next to the giant hinges of the main passage, his face enveloped with concern. The bags present under Frank's eyes betrayed his usual youthful appearance.

The head of security spotted the runaways. "We've . . . everyone . . . particularly your mother has been so worried about you both. Quick! Come in! I need to reseal the gate. Something's going to happen soon," Frank urged as he ushered the children inside. No sooner than the children's heels were through the gate did Frank slam and lock the barrier.

Inside the fortified premises were dozens of security guards. This was unusual compared to the small details that rotated throughout the week. Every sentry from every shift was present. The normally confident units were silent and shaken.

Frank turned to Victoria Schechter and ordered, "Escort Arabella and Maximillian to their mother. She demanded to see them as soon as they were on the grounds. Do not let them out of your sight. For now, they are not allowed to walk the premises without supervision. I'll call back the search and rescue team." Agent Schechter positioned herself in the middle of the two troublemakers and placed a firm hand between the shoulder blades of each. She applied slight pressure forward toward their detainment.

As Frank turned away, he hollered over his shoulder, "Oh, and we've trimmed all the trees adjacent to the perimeter. The only way out is through this gate with my permission."

The long walk across the front lawn felt unusually arduous. The siblings, who were once anxious to get home, were now dragging their feet up the cobblestone driveway. The only thing pushing them forward was Agent Schechter's ever-present hand on their backs. The nearly translucent Lux continued to follow the captives to help them weather their punishment.

Their chaperone quietly opened the large black door and whispered a message to the guard posted inside the entrance. Agent Evans did not speak a word and directed the children to follow him, leading them to the dining room where the customary feast was missing. The only food on the enormous table was two small sandwiches, two pieces of fruit, and two bottles of water. No stemware, plates, or even napkins. All the flourishes were gone.

Before Arabella and Maximillian could even sit, Benjamina flung open the double doors to the dining room. Her face did not betray her worry for the kids. Arabella stood to attention and began, "Mom, who's my—"

Benjamina cut her off. "I don't have time for this. Our world is threatened, and the whole country is counting on me. You're both grounded. Eat, and then go to your rooms." Benjamina reached the other side of the dining room just in time for the children to realize she was just passing through on her way to another briefing.

"Take them to their rooms as soon as they finish eating," she barked at Agent Evans. "Make sure someone is standing guard outside each child's room at all times. I don't want any more incidents today."

The children obediently finished their miniscule portions and rose from the table. Their new custodian gestured for the children to follow once again. Suddenly, a noisy and urgent call came in over the agent's earpiece, so loud that anyone within ten feet could hear the privileged request. "You're not going to believe this. Caius is at the front gate. Get Madame Financier now!"

Agent Evans turned to Arabella and Maximillian. "Get to your rooms. I have to go take care of something. The guards will tell me if you didn't make it." The children were left standing in the vast atrium located in the middle of the manor as the agent sprinted toward the commotion.

"Do they mean Dad?" Maximillian nervously asked Arabella.

"He's not who you think he is. He's coming for me. We need to go," Arabella whispered to her brother.

Juan Flores, Aston Penderbrook, and Clover Bridgewater sat among fellow teachers, first responders, medical professionals, and other community helpers. There were about fifty people in number at the Aurelia City Hall. The group sat silently in a large circle as the weight of the day made it difficult for anyone to speak.

Mr. Flores stood and spoke first, "I call this emergency meeting of The Prominence to order." The teacher paused and wished in this moment he had lesson plans to guide him. The de facto leader would have to galvanize the audience.

"What others believed as folklore, we knew as history. We have spent our lives studying for this day, and we are the most prepared for the upcoming crises."

From memory, Mr. Flores recited the poem but gave special

emphasis to two lines. "One hero from each plane, to bring healing of all pain."

Intently, the novice commander scanned the room. "For the first time, we are able to see the Murk and Animus. We can only assume the Switcher is close, or possibly already here. We must find our hero and protect them. The fate of Aurelia depends on us."

An attendee, vaguely familiar to the assembly, stood and cleared their throat. "I know who you're looking for. You have been protecting her all along. Now you must join her."

21

● ● ●

EUPORIA WAS NOW chaotic, volatile, and dangerous. In under twenty-four hours, the rigid hierarchy was crumbling. The fracture in the atmosphere and the dark beings on the other side had reversed the balance of power. Management was afraid, and everyone else was emboldened. Dez continued to search for Sophia underground, but the tunnels were unusually hectic. Most of the Forgotten were making themselves known above ground, even at this late hour.

A man ran alongside Dez and yelled to his friend across the tunnel, "Come on. I just got word a few groups of techies have some of Management barricaded in their penthouse offices. We don't have much time before more of those filthy managers get to their weapons cache."

The friend responded, "Let's go. We'll grab Darius on the way out. This was a long time coming. If the world is ending, we might as well be a part of it."

Dez couldn't believe her ears; Management was trapped. She wondered what caused this upheaval. *Is this all connected to what just happened in Animus? How does this fit into Author's plan?* Even more determined, Dez knew she needed to find her allies. The heroine wasn't sure how she would find her first collaborator, Sophia, in all of this societal agitation, as dozens of people ran past her with purpose.

The energized teen sprinted, with Lux by her side, through The

Core but did not see a glimpse of the unique vendor. The spirit glided in front of Dez as her personal homing beacon. As she neared the end of the tunnel to above ground, Dez heard the sage voice she was in search of. "Protect yourself. Grab a piece of armor. The oppressors won't go down without a fight."

At the base of the tunnel were massive piles of contraband—bulletproof vests, helmets, and shields. As people ran by the piles toward the fight, they grabbed an item from each mound. Dez had no idea this turbulence was coming, but the Forgotten and their allies had planned on it. Each piece of protective gear was stamped with a yellow, evenly balanced Scale of Justice.

Many of the combatants leaving the tunnel brandished a weapon neutralizer Dez had not seen before. These devices were called demobilizers, nicknamed DeMos, and they were designed to protect the Forgotten from violent Management and their armed guards. The innovative Forgotten, who had been underestimated by E-Corp, had developed highly advanced gloves that sent shock waves to disturb the course of bullets and incapacitate the shooter. The DeMo was expected to be an effective neutralizer but had not been used outside of the testing tunnels. Its activation was designed to be simple; all the user had to do was raise their hands toward their armed aggressor before the trigger was pulled.

As Dez passed the first pile of contraband, Sophia's voice grew louder, shouting numerous instructions. "The elevators are all out in the buildings. You'll have to take the stairs. Be careful. We need each and every one of you to come back safe. The E-Corp Brigade will be everywhere, and they will protect Management at all costs. Violence is their game, not ours. Capture our enemy, and bring them in alive."

After rounding the second large mound of equipment, Sophia's colorful tattooed skin came into view. And not a moment too soon, since Dez's legs were starting to wear. She shouted, "Sophia! I need your help."

Dez and Sophia hurried toward one another and met at the

middle stockpile. The two hugged one another for support. Mid-hug, Sophia whispered in Dez's ear, "I've been waiting for this for a long time. I know more than you think I do. Grab some gear."

Val suddenly awoke. The same explosions and screams from her dreams carried into real life. She jumped from her bed and landed in front of the only window of her studio apartment. The girl pressed her face up against the narrow glass. Peering down onto the street, Val was shocked to see a mangled helicopter on fire. Stoking the blaze were E-Corp uniforms thrown on the crash. Shrieks of terror came from brightly dressed Management as they fled a small mob of drably dressed techies.

Val jumped. Someone was banging on her door. And now the next door. And the next. Part way down the hall, she heard a voice urgently shout, "Down with Management. The Forgotten have gear. Come to The Core. Allies are waiting."

The word *allies* rang in Val's head, even louder than the multiplying footsteps in the hallway. It was not lost on her that this was the second time in one day that someone was requesting allyship. The frightened child wondered where Dez was now.

22

IMMERXIA WAS NOW desperate, isolated, and polarized. In a mere twenty-four hours, the unbelievable reality Immerxians had fabricated was replaced by a reality that was unbelievable. Walter and Caroline spent the last few hours hunkered in the deserted Xitus Library forming a strategy. Walter shared all the information he learned from Author, and Caroline fired off questions until she was out.

Surprisingly, Walter's CommX8 still held a slight charge. Clearly, there had not been any reception in Animus because his communication device repeatedly dinged from all the missed VEXs pouring in. The boy leaned forward so his companion could read the startling communications as well. Lux, their new steward, hovered over their shoulders to discreetly read. Almost all the notifications were trying to locate once-abundant commodities.

> **10:41 P.M. JJBlue:** Anyone know where I can find bread? @GroceryDepot is all out.

> **10:53 P.M. KittyCat47:** I can't find a dynamo anywhere. Do you know if @JouleMart has any?

As the two teens read these unnerving VEXs, even more disturbing ones began to scroll across Walter's CommX8.

11:59 P.M. PhiliptheFox: I'm pretty sure I just saw a ghost in my backyard. Get a load of this! @MiniCam

12:02 A.M. SomethingsOff16: @PhiliptheFox My parents say everyone is overreacting. All this is FAKE! Go check out @OneTrueNews.

12:03 A.M. PhiliptheFox: @SomthingsOff16 I literally just saw it with my own eyes.

12:03 A.M. SomthingsOff16: @PhiliptheFox They're paying you cryptx to share this. You and your friends just want us to be afraid. Wake up people!

1:35 A.M. ImmerxiaChannel7: The President has declared a state of emergency. Everyone is to shelter-in-place. @HomeSecuritySystems

1:35 A.M. OneTrueNews: Don't listen to mainstream media. Come check us out.

1:49 A.M. SaraBeara: Anybody want to come with me and @LLSherlock to find out the truth? @BrightLightFlashlights

2:05 A.M. JerrickKnowsAll: New polls are up! Come take a quiz to find out which phantom you are. Don't forget to check out the redesigned Know-It-All T-shirts.

Walter was disappointed to see his friends' social media idol capitalizing on the unfolding and terrifying events. The VEX further pushed Walter toward his mission of breaking Immerxians from their monetary and material obsessions.

2:17 A.M. MamaWendy: WHERE R U @Walter8? You better be with Pete or Brian! I've sent about a million VEXs to you. Things seem really bad. The whole family is sheltering-in-place. I want a good explanation for not coming home.

Hoping to put his mother's worry at ease and avoid any embarrassing conversations in front of Caroline, Walter VEX'd a quick message to @MamaWendy:

3:21 A.M. Walter8: @MamaWendy I'm safe with a friend at the library. Don't worry. Sorry . . . just got your messages. I'll explain as soon as I get home.

Caroline looked at her neglected phone and noticed she had multiple missed calls from her parents, Beverly and Barry. She listened to the last voice message from her mom.

"Hi, honey. Just wanted to make sure you were alright. Your father and I tracked your phone to the library. I bet you fell asleep there again. Stay there until we know what's going on. Call me when you get this. You better not leave the library until we give you the all clear. Okay? Love you!"

Caroline quickly ended the voicemail and hoped Walter had not heard the embarrassing message. She excused herself from the table to call and relieve her parents' worries. Once Caroline returned, Walter said, "Let's get a list together of friends we trust and think will help us."

"Well, this is easy for me. My list is pretty short. I have a good friend, Cam, that sees the same doctor as me. I know she'll be interested in portals to other worlds and supernatural beings. She considers herself an aspiring scientist, so she'll want to investigate and determine if the world is much larger than she once knew."

"What's her last name? I can look her up in Global Messaging. I'll include her in a private group chat I'm setting up. I'm going to invite Brian, Pete, and Carrie. I think Carrie will join us because of what she saw in the cafeteria yesterday." Walter was already fast at work on his CommX8.

"Cam's last name is Nguyen. Do you really think people will join us?" Caroline pondered out loud.

"We have to believe they will," Walter stated with conviction.

The adolescents crafted their appeal.

To: @GreenJewel, @BriGuy100, @the_Pete, @Carrielovescritters

3:42 A.M. Walter8: Need help! Meet me and Caroline at the library. ASAP! Explain when you get here.

3:42 A.M. BriGuy100: My parents are really freaked out. Not sure if they'll let me leave the house. None of us have slept. I'll try to get there as soon as I can.

3:44 A.M. GreenJewel: Anything for Caroline. Let me get dressed. My parents got called in to work, so I can be there in five.

3:45 A.M. the_Pete: Heard there's phantoms on Main Street. What do you need help with? I don't feel like risking my life for nothing.

3:45 A.M. Walter8: I know what's going on in Immerxia, and I know how to stop it.

3:45 A.M. the_Pete: That sounds like something. I'll sneak out of the house in a sec.

3:55 A.M. Carrielovescritters: I'm freaked out right now, but after what I saw you do yesterday at lunch, I'm on my way. My parents are glued to the TV.

3:55 A.M. Walter8: Be careful. There are forces at work that don't want you to get here.

The newsroom was buzzing. The meteorologists, anchors, and producers struggled to sift through the barrage of reports of strange phenomena. Unverified reports of disruptions in the atmosphere exposing creatures trying to break into the world were increasing by the minute. Consequently, the earth was shaking everywhere, and tension was building among the terrified citizens.

The lead producer corralled the early morning news team.

"Listen up. We've got a lot to report and only an hour to do it. Our viewers need information, accurate information."

Looking to the chief meteorologist, the producer ordered, "We're opening with you at the top of the hour. You have to explain these tremors to the audience. Make clear they are not earthquakes, but we think they are related to the visions in the air. Only state what you know. Our credibility is on the line."

The producer then turned her attention to the lead anchor. "Obviously, we don't know what is happening, but it's your job to calm the viewers. Guns are flying off the racks, and food is in short supply. People are preparing for the worst. Try to talk them back off the ledge. If things grow much worse, violence will ensue."

Speaking to the graphics supervisor, the producer warned, "We have tons of visuals to show. You won't need to loop any of the same videos. Our reporters continue to send new material. Screen the content in real time and play the most attention-grabbing clips. Make sure to put the *disturbing content* warning up the entire hour."

The producer ended with, "Look alive. This could be our most important show ever."

A reporter in another room of the station called with a nervous intensity over the intercom, "Shawn is on the line, and he needs more cameramen as soon as possible. He has a visual on hundreds of the creatures."

EPILOGUE

MOST OF ANIMUS no longer resembled Pax, save for the garden that Author enjoyed creating from. The blooming plot of land contained an array of flora and fauna, including two plants and animals from every species. All life harmoniously coexisted in this one garden, creating the most beautiful landscape imaginable. There were flowering plants, spreading ground cover, and towering trees. And all were flourishing. There were furry beasts, scaly critters, and unimaginably small crawlies. And all breathed easy. Author sat in the middle of the garden next to a cluster of Perpetua, a near-extinct floweret that had a deep black stem and matching petals. Dew that touched the flowering Perpetua turned the bloom brilliant white.

Knowing the importance of completing the work, Author stepped away from the fight and sat on a columnar pile of thick books. The self-authored collection of manuscripts rose from the soil as if it were another species of plant. In Author's lap sat an almost completed leatherbound volume. Author spun Calamus, recently wielded against the Murk, in hand. Deep in thought, Author did not even notice the worsening winds bending the trees. After much contemplation and with earnestness, Author put pen to paper and wrote:

"There's so much more to go. There's so much more to give. But there's so much more to gain. Believe."

From Animus, the Switcher coolly watched Author's Intrepid Three hastily formulate a plan in their separate planes. Just as before, the predator stalked its prey through the perceptibly thin atmosphere. There were no Lumen in sight to guard the weak barrier; the humans had never been more vulnerable. The surviving Lumen were assuredly scrambling to recover from the heavy casualties their ranks suffered.

Panning from one plane to the next, the Switcher heard the building chaos of sirens, shouts, and cries. It felt a swell of pride. Hubris turned to contemplation.

"People. They are what I always hoped. Vessels of destruction," the Switcher said aloud. "The moment Author gave them free will, my victory was assured, and their defeat was sealed. Weak. Weak. Weak. Why put any trust in such a feeble creation?

"With freedom came consequences. Soon people will face the fallout of their actions, and they are so ill-equipped. They spent so much time searching for the inequities of others that they missed their own. The little whisper inside them has been mine for centuries. They will be so surprised to see how foul they've been. They will crumble and fall. How wonderful! I have waited lifetimes to watch their ultimate destruction. The time has finally come to complete their demise.

"The humans may put up a fight, they love to fight, but they are used to petty squabbles, not true war. This will neither be petty nor a squabble. They won't last long. The divided never do. People do not care for one another; they may not even care for themselves. Their disdain for their own kind is an asset to my Murk and me.

"Author thinks the creation is so magnificent, but my manipulation proves otherwise. The proof is everywhere. Surely, this is not the outcome my enemy designed. How silly to use children. The *Intrepid* Three have much to fear. There is no amount of light that could ignite this fading world. Darkness will prevail."

ACKNOWLEDGMENTS

THANK YOU TO our parents, Doug and Rita Crockett and Mark and Robin Penfold, your time, love, and support have always been and will always be invaluable. A special thank you to Doug, Rita, and Robin for being our very first readers and sounding boards.

Thank you to Ignacio Ocaranza and Jordan Bristow for visualizing these new and fantastical places with us.

Thank you to Mylina Russell for helping us develop our image as authors.

Thank you to Brandon Russell for reading our book and giving such thoughtful and valuable feedback.

Thank you to John Koehler and the Koehler Book team for taking a chance on us as emerging authors.

Lastly, thank you to the family and friends that came before us, the ones that walked beside us, and the ones that supported and challenged us along our way. You helped make this dream come true.

CPSIA information can be obtained
at www.ICGtesting.com
Printed in the USA
BVHW071257310523
665081BV00003B/411